MARRYING
Mr. Valentine

Laura Barnard
AMAZON BESTSELLING AUTHOR

Dedication

This book is dedicated to my gorgeous cousin Megan. Always my faithful companion at signings, the book world wouldn't be the same without you and your shenanigans by my side.

Love you lots x

Chapter 1

Tuesday 2nd January

'It's off. The wedding; it's cancelled,' she sniffs down the phone.

Crap. I've barely gotten to my desk after the Christmas break and already I've got Miss Samson calling with a cancellation. I've never had this happen before. Especially with only a little over a month before the wedding. I suppose that's shocking considering I've been doing this for over a year.

'Oh, I'm so sorry,' I say as delicately as I can, 'and you're one hundred percent sure you want to cancel? You don't want to have a think about it? You realise you'll lose your deposit...'

I have heard the Christmas period is the most stressful time for couples. Thank God, I don't have a stupid man to argue with.

'Fuck the deposit!' she snaps, so loudly I have to hold the phone away from my ear. 'He's been shagging his secretary. He gave me herpes! It's as black and white as that.'

What a happy new year she's having.

'Oh dear. Well, okay. I'm so sorry. If I can find someone to take your place, I'll speak to my boss about possibly refunding your deposit.' It should be simple enough. We have a two-year waiting list.

'Oh, Nadine,' she sighs with another sniff. 'I'm going to miss you. You've been so helpful. I feel as if we've become friends.'

'Me too.'

I hope she doesn't ask me out for a drink or anything. That would be weird. Of course, I come across as the perfect friend when she's paying me, but I don't have time in my life for another friend. I have enough trouble keeping up with the ones I have.

'Well, thanks for everything, Nadine. Goodbye.'

Right. Some bride-to-be is going to have her day made and have her wedding on the 3rd February. I scan my hand down the list. A Miss Blumenkrantz and Mr Valentine. I punch in the numbers.

'Hello,' a female voice answers hastily, already sounding like I'm a PPI caller she's eager to dismiss. Little does she know I'm about to make her year.

'Hello Miss Blumenkrantz, I have some potential good news for you.'

Thursday 4th January

The couple are coming in today for our first meeting. It's where I would usually learn more about them and get a general gist of how they want their wedding. But that's when we're usually about two years in advance of the wedding. With just over a month to plan this, I'm going to have to go a bit more in depth and get this show on the road.

I look up at the sound of the door banging to see a tall blonde—only slightly shorter than me—waltz in with all the confidence in the world. She flicks her perfectly tousled hair behind her shoulder. She looks like a Hollywood movie star.

'Hi, I'm Miss Blumenkrantz. I assume you're Nadine?' She starts undoing her double-breasted cobalt-blue coat. It looks expensive.

'Yes.' I stand and shake her hand, trying not to look intimidated. Wow, she nearly pulls my arm out of the socket. That's one strong handshake. 'Glad to meet you.'

'The pleasure's mine,' she nods with a wide smile. 'Call me Clara. I can't tell you how happy I am that a date came up. Everyone is talking about this place.'

'Yes,' I nod. 'We were named best wedding venue of 2017 by Confetti Bride,' I add proudly.

'I heard. My cousin actually owns the venue.'

I frown. 'Your cousin? Do you mean Hugh?'

Hugh is my best friend, Florence's, husband. They got married here themselves just a year ago on Christmas day and he surprised her by buying the place.

'Yes, that's him. Daddy prefers to keep our money in the family, so he's over the moon Hugh bought the venue of my dreams.'

Daddy? God, she's a posh bird. Generally, anyone over the age of eleven that still calls their dad "Daddy" is either rich or has mental health issues. Jesus, what a small world with Hugh being her cousin. I'll have to be careful as fuck with this one. If anything goes wrong, Hugh will kick my arse. Of all the people on the waiting list I had to call his cousin to get married in a month.

I can't help but notice that Mr Valentine's not here yet.

'I'm sorry, I thought you were bringing your fiancé too? I normally find it good to meet both of you. It gives me a better idea of you guys as a couple.'

She waves her hand towards the door. 'He's just parking the car. He'll be in soon.'

As if right on cue, the door opens and in walks an absolute god of a man. That's the only way to describe him. He's got longish blonde hair, long enough to tie back into a roughly put up top knot that I would normally despise. Only he easily carries it off. He has the broadest shoulders I've ever seen and a jaw so square he could be made of Lego.

Fuck me, he's fit. Where the hell did she find him? He's like a sexy Viking.

I quickly look down at my paperwork to hide my blushes. Of course, I'm used to meeting good looking men in this line of work, but this guy is like nothing else I've ever seen. He could be a model, but I doubt he is. He looks too manly to want to prance around in his underwear. What a shame for the UK population of women.

He doesn't look her type. She's posh and business-like, whereas he looks casual and strong. God, he could be a lumberjack with a body like that. I'd watch him take down a tree any day. Or take a look at his wood if you know what I mean. Jesus, how did my thoughts get so filthy so quickly?

'Hey,' he says to her, his voice low and husky.

Fuck, if it was possible to come from just hearing a voice I'd be screaming like a crazy person right now. I must really need to get some.

She pats the seat beside her. 'Come on, darling. Nadine here was just talking to us about things.'

He juggles his keys and eventually puts them in his trouser back pocket before making himself comfortable on the chair. It's only then that he looks at me. His eyes widen for a split second, as if shocked by something, but he quickly recovers. Do I have something in my teeth?

'So, what kind of things?' he asks, looking me dead in the eye. God, he's got the most amazing forest-green eyes, with just a hint of hazel around the edges. I feel my body heat as they search my face.

Clearing my throat in a desperate attempt to pull myself together, I place my hands on the desk to try to stop them shaking.

'I'd just like an idea of what you have in mind for your special day.'

He snorts and rolls his eyes. 'Best ask my fiancée. She's the one steaming ahead with it all.'

Steaming ahead with it all? They've been on the waiting list for over eight months. I'd hardly say that's rushing things. Shame he sounds like a non-committal prick. I wonder if that's why she's not accepted a cancellation before now?

She protrudes her eyes at him, as if warning him to shut up, before quickly looking back to me with a smile.

'What he's trying to say, is that I'm handling all of the minor details. I'm thinking a black and white theme. Very glamourous, sophisticated. Almost art deco.'

I nod along, deliberately trying not to look at the sexy eyes on his glorious face. 'Okay. That sounds like something we can do. I'll just write down some particulars.'

'Actually, I have a better idea,' she interrupts.

What is it about this woman that tells me she's going to be hard work? She's high maintenance from the tip of her Louboutin's to the top of her perfectly highlighted hair.

'Really?' I ask with a pleasant smile I long since learned to master.

She claps her hands together. 'You simply *have* to come to our engagement party. That way you can see my sense of style for yourself.'

'Oh... okay.'

I'm not used to clients inviting me out to things. Most of them have already celebrated their engagement by the time they come to me. It doesn't really make sense that they'd only be having an engagement party now.

'So, you're just having an engagement party now, even though you've been engaged for...?' I look around in my notes, but I don't have that specific information.

'We've only been engaged for a month,' Mr Valentine says.

'Oh.' I frown. 'It's just that I've had you on the waiting list for eight months.'

He frowns back at me before turning to her. 'What is she going on about?'

She rolls her eyes. 'Well, naturally, darling, I suspected for a while now that you were going to propose. So, I just... made sure we were giving ourselves a fighting chance securing the place.'

'Before I've even seen the venue?' he asks, clearly horrified. 'What if I hated it?'

She rolls her eyes, a dismissing smile on her lips. 'Sweets, it won best venue in 2017. What more is there to know?'

He drags his hand through his hair, clearly counting to

ten. I get a feeling he does that a lot.

She smiles, pleased he's been put to rest. 'So, I'll email you the details of the engagement party.'

I smile. What is it about this couple that tells me this isn't going to be your normal wedding?

Chapter 2

Friday 5th January

'I can't believe I got talked into attending this engagement party,' I whine to my best mate Florence down the phone as the taxi pulls up outside their venue.

I'm beyond tired after overseeing today's wedding at the pub. The couple had a Harry Potter theme, so I've left Dumbledore in charge for the rest of the evening. Hugh promised he'd lock up later.

'Just don't go. It's going above and beyond your job role.'

I laugh. 'You know me. I'll either do it one-hundred-and-ten-percent or not bother at all.'

I do wish I was able to say no sometimes though. It would get me out of these stupid scenarios.

'Well in this case, I think you should not bother at all.

Would it have been so bad for you to have that weekend off?' she sighs. 'We could have booked a spa trip!' She shrieks down the phone comically.

I sigh, as I thank the Uber driver. 'You know I can never relax at those things, so what's the point?'

I really don't see the point in just sitting around in robes with absolutely nothing to do. I'd go stir crazy. It sounds more stressful to me.

'All I'm saying, is that you should give yourself a break. Remember, we don't need the extra business. We're completely booked up for the next two years.'

I nod, a smug smile she can't see gracing my face. 'Yes, and that's because I put everything I have into every wedding.'

'Okay,' she says on a sigh, clearly not believing me. 'Whatever you say.'

'Anyway, I was half expecting to find out you were coming too, with it being Hugh's cousin.'

'Afraid not, love muffin. I've been working all day at a shoot and I'm knackered. Hugh's going though. He's just getting ready now, so I'll tell him to look out for you. I still think you work too hard.'

I look up at the swanky wine bar that's been hired for the event. It's completely the opposite to our rustic barn venue, but she clearly knows what she wants. I can't see anyone arguing with her. Ever. I wonder what she does for a living?

'Trust me. It's still easier than teaching.'

I taught reception class for ten years, but I was more than ready for the career move. Whoever said teaching is so rewarding has clearly not had to deal with five-year-olds shitting themselves.

'Well, at least try to have fun tonight.' She starts giggling. 'Hugh, stop it, I'm on the phone.'

God, those two are gross. It's been a year. You'd think they'd have gotten over the honeymoon period by now. But then I suppose they did only meet a month before getting married. Not exactly your normal scenario. I end the call without saying goodbye.

I pull my shoulders back and brace myself. Show time.

I walk in with a forced confident smile. It drops off my face as soon as I realise how opulent it is here.

The walls are painted a glossy black. Huge golden mirrors adorn the walls with liquor stacked on shelves against them. The bar is gold; the bar stools a grey velvet. Okay, this place is bloody swanky.

The worst thing is that everyone seems to be in cocktail dresses. Yet, here I am in just my smart jeans, and heels—from New Look. There isn't a single heel here that isn't painted red. A cheapy in a sea of Louboutin's. One woman turns, dressed in a silver frock that clings to her tiny body, and gives me a look of disdain. *Hmm, nice friends.*

'There you are, Nadine!' I look up to see Clara walking towards me, her arms out as if to embrace me.

You'd think I'd be used to all this kissy-kissy stuff being in the wedding business, but I'm not. Rich people make me itch. She pulls me in, squishing her cheek against mine and making a kissing noise, rather than connecting her lips.

'You have to come and meet my father.'

I smile, even though she didn't seem to pause to consider if I wanted to. I haven't even got a drink yet. Not that I can probably afford the prices here. I might have to put it on my credit card.

Her father is the brother to Hugh's horrendous mother, whose company I had to endure during their wedding. How I didn't bitch slap that old cow I'll never know. I'm *such* a good friend.

She pulls me towards a man of only about five-feet-eight, with greying hair. So far, he looks nothing like Hugh's mother. Let's hope he's not as evil.

'Daddy, this is our wedding planner, Nadine.'

He takes my hand and shakes it violently. Ah, so that's where she gets her handshake from.

'Good to meet you, Nadine. I hope you're looking after my Princess here.' He smiles fondly at her as if she were still a six-year-old girl.

I force a smile, hoping it isn't a grimace. 'Of course.'

'That's good to hear. I'm told by my nephew, Hugh, that you're an excellent planner.'

I'm actually the manager, but whatever. If he wants to refer to me as a wedding planner so be it. Most people do.

He turns to Clara. 'Where has Hartley got to?'

Hartley. What an unusual name. It suits him.

She rolls her eyes. 'Oh, he's around here somewhere sulking.'

'Sulking?' her father asks, a line having appeared between his eyebrows. 'Why on earth is he sulking? I've given him permission to take your hand. He should be the happiest man on the planet.'

Err... maybe he's met her? It'd take a complete saint not to have second thoughts.

Hartley's suddenly walking past, looking delicious in a navy wool suit with a crisp, white, open-necked shirt. Clara leans out and wraps her hand firmly around his wrist. 'Here he is.' She leans in and gives him a quick kiss on the cheek.

'Hartley, my daughter here says you're sulking. I hope that's not the case?' There's warning in his voice. He's definitely related to Hugh's mother.

'No, Sir,' he says with a smile that doesn't meet his eyes. 'Just a bit stressed out with work. That's all.' Now I look at him closer he does seem stressed, his jaw tense and those glorious eyes troubled.

Clara's father rolls his eyes. 'You see, Nadine,' he explains, swilling his whiskey around, 'Hartley here insists on being a schoolteacher.' He scoffs, as if the very idea is hilarious.

No way. He's a teacher? How have I not bumped into him over the years?

I look at Hartley with new admiration. He might be marrying this piece of work, but he's a teacher. He must have some good in him.

'I understand, actually,' I say with a smile. 'I used to be a teacher too. It's a very demanding job.'

Hartley frowns. '*You* were a teacher?'

Why does he sound so astonished? Why the hell wouldn't he think I was ever a teacher? Am I not maternal seeming or something? I can't help but be offended. He might as well have called me unfeminine.

'Yep,' I nod, rocking awkwardly on my heels. 'I only gave it up just over a year ago to do this job.'

Clara shakes her head. 'I have no idea why Hartley insists on spending time with those little twerps.' She curls her lip up as if she's smelt bad fish. 'Kids are disgusting.'

That's a pretty broad statement.

'Do you not want kids of your own, Clara?' I can't help but ask. I know it's nosy, but I just find it unusual for a woman to talk about kids with nothing but contempt.

'God, no!' she laughs. 'If I wanted something that cries and poops I'd have got a dog. At least you can put them in kennels without being reported.' She laughs hysterically, slapping her thigh, clearly finding herself hilarious.

'Well,' her father says, eager to change the subject, 'I keep telling him that he should come and work for my company. Earn some real money, but will he listen?'

Hartley's jaw tenses further, but he forces another

insincere smile. 'Why would I need to earn lots of money, when you have enough for both of us?'

I burst out laughing. Clara looks appalled. We both look to her dad for his reaction.

He slaps Hartley on the back. 'There's that fun sense of humour I know my daughter loves.' He seems to wave at someone away from us. 'Anyway, I have to go. Just seen an old business associate.'

He walks off and I watch as Hartley's body physically relaxes. He clearly doesn't like the dude. God, imagine having him as a father-in-law? Him and Florence will definitely bond after marrying into this nightmare family.

'So what year do you teach?' I ask him, glad I've been handed a subject I excel at.

'I teach drama at a high school.' Ah, that would make sense as to why I've never bumped into him before. Different age group. You couldn't pay me to teach hormonal adolescents. I'd take the whiny five-year-olds any day.

'Hugh!' Clara squeals, opening her arms wide, looking behind me.

I turn to see Hugh rushing towards her.

'Hi, Clara,' he says, giving her an affectionate hug. He's smiling, but I notice it doesn't meet his eyes either. Those creases I'm used to seeing whenever he smiles affectionately at Florence just aren't there.

Could it be that he can't stand her either? It would make sense. Hugh is nothing like her.

He shakes Hartley's hand, slapping him on the back.

'Hi, Hartley.' He nods a hello at me. 'Sorry to interrupt you guys. What were you talking about?'

Clara puts her hand on Hartley's shoulder possessively. 'Hartley was telling us how stressed he is at work. I keep telling him he should come work for Daddy.'

Hartley rolls his eyes.

'Well,' Hugh says with a smile, 'I can understand him wanting to stay in a job he has a passion for.'

'Thank you,' Hartley says, pointing at him as if to show Hugh gets it. 'I'm normally not as hard-pressed, but the teacher helping me put on a play has just been signed off on early maternity leave.'

'That can't be helped, darling,' Clara says, inspecting her nails as if bored. 'Although if these breeders stopped for a minute and thought about other people, maybe they'd have fewer children.'

I ignore her comment. I wouldn't know where to start with a response to that. I'd probably just headbutt her.

'Must be a big workload for one person though,' I sympathise to Hartley. It's hard enough being a teacher, it's even worse when under-staffed.

'Wait!' Clara says, clapping her hands together, her eyes lit up. 'Why don't you help him?'

'Sorry?' we both say at the same time.

She beams, as if she's had the best idea ever. 'You used to be a teacher. I'm sure you'd love to see some kids again, to get involved with a school production like this one. And it'll help you two to get to know each other.'

'Babe,' he warns with a tight smile. 'I'm sure Nadine is very busy with weddings.'

I'm just about to agree and say 'thanks, but no thanks' when Hugh steps forward. Bless him, he's going to stand up for me.

'Nadine would love to!' he says, grinning at me with warning in his eyes. What the hell is he doing?

'Oh... I mean...' I start. Hartley looks at me hopefully. I should really say no. But... well, the people pleaser in me is desperate to help. 'I suppose I could spare a few hours this week. I've done most of the prep for this weekend's wedding.'

'Sounds great,' Hugh agrees enthusiastically.

Hartley doesn't seem too sure. Maybe he doesn't want my help? I am, after all, just some random woman he's just met.

'But I mean, only if you're desperate.' I want to give him the chance to turn me down and you know... get out of it.

'I am,' he nods. 'But only if you don't mind. I feel bad taking up your time. Don't feel you have to say yes.'

I open my mouth to speak but Clara jumps in for me. 'Of course, she doesn't mind.'

'That's settled then,' Hugh says with a definite nod.

I nod too, already dreading it.

'Ah, and here is my grandma now,' Clara says. 'My namesake.'

I turn to see an elderly woman with rosy cheeks and tight-set brown curls walking towards us in an elegant mint blouse and black trousers. I recognise her from Hugh and Florence's wedding last year.

'Grandma, this is Nadine. She's planning our wedding at The Duck and Goose.'

Her face lights up in recognition. 'Ah, yes. Nadine, best friend of our Florence.'

Florence has always talked highly of the woman, so there's no need for me to be scared, but there's something about her regal presence that intimidates me.

'Nice to meet you,' I say, doing a ridiculous curtesy. Jesus, Nads, she's not the queen.

She smiles kindly. 'I've heard you're a wonderful wedding planner. The day should be gorgeous.'

I suddenly worry that Florence will have told her my history. The air in here feels limited, like the oxygen is being sucked out. I need to leave. Get outside and force a bit of fresh air into my lungs.

'Anyway, it was lovely to meet you, but I'm afraid I'm going to have to go,' I say with an apologetic smile. 'I have another event I have to go to.'

An event at club bed with DJ pillow.

'Ah, well, you'll be missed,' Clara says, already waving to someone else she sees. Yeah, right.

'I'll walk you out,' Hugh says, taking my arm.

He obviously wants to talk to me. As soon as I'm outside, I gasp in a lungful of air and sit down on the step.

'Shit, Nads, are you okay?' he asks, rushing to hold my shoulder back.

'I'm fine,' I insist, counting back from ten in my head. 'Just a bit smoky in there.'

He raises his eyebrows.

Oh yeah, I keep forgetting I can't use that excuse since the smoking ban. It's been over ten years, Nadine. Get the fuck with it.

'What the hell is going on, Hugh?' I ask, as soon as my breathing has started to go back to normal; my heart no longer feeling like it's trying to escape my ribcage. 'Why are you volunteering me to work in a school?'

'I'm sorry about that,' he says, a slight sheen of sweat I hadn't noticed before on his forehead. 'But I need to keep Uncle Charlie sweet.'

'There's keeping him sweet and then sucking his arse. I mean, of course we'll give them the best wedding we can in a month, but why are you acting so jumpy?'

He sighs, a frown marring his face as he sits down on the step next to me. 'Look, my uncle invested money in the company.'

'Huh? Clara's dad? He's a partner?' How is it I didn't know this before?

'Not so much a partner, as an investor. I didn't want

to ask my dad for the money and I needed it quickly, so they didn't sell the pub to the other developers.'

Ah, yes, I do remember the reason he bought the pub in the first place. They were planning to sell it to developers who were going to knock it down and build flats. Something Hugh normally does himself, but he couldn't see the place he got married be destroyed, so he bought it instead.

'So, Uncle Charlie lent me the money. I've got a repayment plan with him, but he's been extremely reasonable with his interest rates. He's told me he expects the red carpet rolled out for Clara.'

'Why are you so scared of him?'

He rubs at his eyes as if the weight of the world is on his shoulders. 'Because I don't want him to tell my dad he leant me the money. He'd probably disown me from the shame that I didn't go to him.'

'Okay,' I nod. 'I'm starting to get it. But can't you just take out another mortgage and pay him back?'

He sighs. 'No. You know I'm mortgaged to the hilt, what with our place and the latest flat development. They should all be sold in the next few months and then I'll be able to pay him back, but until then I need to keep him sweet.'

Shit. I had no idea they were in such a scary financial situation. I always just thought of Hugh as rich.

'So that means us pulling out all the stops, including making sure Hartley is not stressed.'

'Meaning I'm on babysitting duty,' I nod with a sigh.

'Afraid so. But don't worry.' He takes me by the shoulders. 'I have every faith in you.'

Saturday 6th January

I'm lucky enough that I have responsible staff I've managed to train up and mould into trustworthy employees, but that doesn't stop me coming to every wedding and checking everything is in order. Call it the control freak in me. You could call it me having no life, but I take my work seriously.

Florence is always ribbing me about it, and Hugh's always on my case to take more of a step back, but I just can't. I've only been working here a year and I know that if I wasn't such a control freak, it wouldn't have won that award. There's no way it would have gone from such strength to strength.

So many people in the wedding industry seem to be replaced within a couple of months as they're on internships from universities. I've even had three brides willingly lose their deposits in order to change their venue to us because they've heard about the sincerely personable service we offer.

Anyway, that's how I find myself with my clipboard checking off everything to make sure this wedding is running perfectly. The bride is in the bridal suite which is basically what used to be the flat above the pub. Only now we've re-decorated it into a fabulous shabby-chic penthouse with enough room for the bride to get ready, along with her bridesmaids.

With only an hour before the wedding I decide to check in on the bride. I walk up the stairs and knock on the door. There seems to be a lot of commotion coming from the other side. I find this a lot. Bridesmaids seem to bicker just before walking down the aisle. I think it's caused from the fear of all those people staring at them.

The door finally opens, revealing a distressed looking bridesmaid in a lavender, silk dressing gown, her hair in curlers.

'Hi. I'm just checking in to see if everything is going okay?' I ask and follow with a professional smile.

'Ugh.' She grabs me by my forearms and drags me in. 'We've had a fucking disaster!'

Oh Jesus. Just what I want on a Sunday. Thank God, I came in.

'What's happened?' I ask as I'm dragged into the main room.

The bride is stood next to her dress, hysterical, with tears rolling down her face. The bridesmaids are hurrying around the dress attempting to wipe at it with a wet cloth.

'What's happened to the dress?' I ask, already going in the emergency cupboard for the baby wipes. There isn't much that these bad boys won't get out. Not my first stained dress situation.

The girls disperse so I can see the damage done to it.

My mouth drops open of its own accord. Sweet mother of all that is holy!

The bottom half has bloodstains all over it. What the hell has happened?

'Shit, did...' I look from bridesmaid to bridesmaid, gulping down the bile. 'Did... someone die here?'

One bridesmaid doubles over laughing. Oh, okay, hopefully that means they haven't. That or she's a dark bitch who finds murder funny. I'm faithful to my clients but covering up a murder is a step too far.

'I came on my period,' the bride explains in between sobs. 'God, I shouldn't have been due on for at least another two weeks. And now my whole wedding is ruined!'

Well this is a first. I've never even had to lend a bride a tampon before. Mother nature is a right bitch.

I quickly open my phone and type in *'how to get blood out of fabric'*. An article pops up straight away. Thank god for Google. How did people ever cope before the internet?

'Okay, we need to wash it with soap and cold water. Then dab on some ammonia.'

'Ammonia?' the bride repeats. 'Where the hell are we going to get that?'

She's right. I have no idea what ammonia is, let alone where to get it from. Not that I can show them I'm panicking.

I smile assuredly. 'I'll go into town and buy some. Meanwhile call around all of your friends and family and see if they can get any.'

The bride stands in front of me, her lip trembling. 'But what if you can't get any?'

I scoff confidently. 'I'll be able to find some. Don't worry about a thing.'

I run down the stairs, grab my coat and get into my car, dialling Florence. Thank God, she's my number one on speed dial.

'Hey, babe,' she says down the phone, munching on what sounds like toast. 'You okay?'

'No.' I cry dramatically. 'The bride has bloody had her period on her dress, so I'm headed into town to try to buy some ammonia.'

'Bloody hell! Pun intended.' She collapses into giggles.

I roll my eyes. Real bloody helpful Flo.

'You don't have any, do you?'

She scoffs. 'Ammonia? As if! I couldn't even tell you if it's a liquid or a powder.'

'Fuck.' I sigh, feeling the weight of the world on my shoulders. 'Would you meet me in town? I have to somehow find it. Or I'll have to find something else for her to wear.'

'Fuck.' I hear the panic in her voice for me. Bless her. 'Of course. I'll quickly get dressed and meet you there.'

I feel bad for causing her to rush on a Sunday, but I'm desperate at this point. Every staff member here needs to stay to get on with their jobs, so she's literally the only one capable of helping me.

***

By the time Flo finds me, I've already gone into three shops looking for ammonia. Each time a bewildered shop assistant asks me what that is. Fucking morons. That's what happens when you employ fourteen-year-olds with no knowledge. Read a book for Christ's sake!

Okay, so it's fair to say I'm a little fraught and sweaty. I've been gone for twenty minutes and I still have no solution to the wedding taking place in forty minutes. This woman cannot cancel her wedding just because mother nature has decided to fuck her over. I refuse to let it happen. She's paying us enough to make this my problem too.

'What the hell are we going to do?' Flo asks, her eyes darting from side to side.

I think for a minute, pinching my temples as if to help pull my thoughts together. Sometimes I really wish I had superpowers.

'Okay, we're gonna have to go to a bridal shop and hope to fuck they can help us.'

'Right,' Flo nods, but I don't miss her large gulp. 'That's totally doable.' She takes my hand. 'Come on.'

We practically run into the first shop, my hair now

stuck to my head with sweat.

'I need a dress!' I shout at the lady behind the till.

Her eyes widen to twice the size.

'Of course you do,' she says with a smarmy smile, 'but I'm afraid that you need an appointment.'

I don't have time for this basic bitch right now.

'I want to speak to your manager. Now. We're in a hurry.'

She scoffs but goes out back. Thirty-three seconds later—yes, I counted—a lady with auburn hair tied up in a tight bun comes walking out. She's so lithe she must have been a ballerina earlier in life. Her shoulders are squared, as if ready for a fight.

I put on my nicest smile.

'Hi. I'm Nadine Roberts, wedding organiser from The Duck and Goose, winner of Best Wedding Venue 2017.'

This seems to get her attention, her eyes widening a fraction for a split second before she quickly covers it with an impassive face.

'Lovely to meet you, Nadine. We've had many a recommendation here from you.'

'Yes, you have,' I nod. 'Only I have a problem. An emergency really, and I need you to pull out all of the stops to help me.'

'Okay,' she nods, suspicious. 'What can I do for you?'

'I need a wedding dress to take right now.'

'Right now?' she repeats in horror. 'By the end of

today? Are you serious?'

'Nope.' She relaxes slightly. 'As in something I can take in the next ten minutes.'

'You're pulling my leg,' she says on a laugh. 'Is this some kind of a joke?'

'We wish it was,' Flo says, 'but apparently the bride bled all over hers.'

The woman puts her hand to her chest aghast. 'Bled? Has there been some kind of murder?'

Jesus, with the drama queens in this industry. Me being one of them.

'No, she's started her period.'

The whole shop seems to have fallen silent, brides looking at me in revulsion.

'Yeah, yeah. I said period, ladies.' I scream, having apparently lost my shit. 'We all have them. We have it in common. No need to look so appalled.'

The woman takes my arm. 'Please.' She pulls me to the side of the shop. 'If you stop scaring my customers, I'll find something that can help.'

'Excellent.'

Turns out acting like a psychopath works sometimes. I should pull that act out of the bag more often.

'What size is your bride?'

'She's a small size twelve.' I look over Florence. 'She's about the same height as her.'

She nods. 'Okay. It'll have to be a sample dress. I'm

thinking ideally a corset back. That way you can make it looser or tighter depending on her back width.'

'Yes, great. But we need it, like ten minutes ago.'

She rushes off, summoning the basic bitch behind the desk with a click of her fingers. She glares at me. Yeah, yeah, run along now.

♡♡♡

Florence and I run into the pub with only five minutes until the wedding is due to start; guests are making their way to the barn. We politely push them out of the way and run up the stairs of the pub and into the flat. Four fully dressed up, depressed looking bridesmaids turn to stare at us in hope.

'We have a dress!' I shout triumphantly, holding the dress bag in the air like a trophy.

The bride's face transforms from morose to an expression of absolute relief. She runs over, snatching the dress bag from my hands.

'Oh my God, Nadine. I could kiss you.'

I blush. 'No need. Just get your arse in this dress in the next three minutes.'

The bridesmaids start fussing over her, helping to secure her in it. Thankfully she's so grateful she doesn't seem to mind that it's a slightly different style. If she'd have complained, I'd have probably had to punch her and that wouldn't go down well. I can just see the newspaper headlines now: *'Wedding Planner punches Bride-to-Be with minutes before Wedding'.* That's one way to commit career suicide.

I turn to see Flo leaning against the wall, her face unusually pale. I'm just about to ask her if she's okay when her eyes flutter and then she's sliding down the floor onto her bum.

I rush over, glad her eyes aren't completely closed.

'Shit, Flo. Are you okay?' She doesn't answer me, her breath coming out in short spurts. 'Someone get some water.' I shout to the bridesmaids.

One brings a glass of water over just as Flo's eyes begin to open fully again. She looks around as if not sure what just happened.

'Flo. Should I call an ambulance?'

She shakes her head, taking the water from the bridesmaid. She takes a large gulp.

'I'm fine,' she dismisses. 'I'm just tired. So I think I'm gonna go home.'

Is she crazy? The woman almost passed out.

'I'll drive you. But first you're drinking that water, having some food and resting for a little while longer. Otherwise I'm going to force you to the hospital.'

The bride thanks us, now ready in her dress, and hurries off past us to get married.

I eventually drive Flo home, the colour finally back in her cheeks.

'What the hell happened back there?' I ask as we finally pull into her road.

'I had a few too many wines last night. All the rushing around made me feel hungover. I just need to get to bed.'

'Okay. Have a good sleep hun.'

But something tells me she's lying. About what I have no idea.

Chapter 3

Monday 8th January

I'm helping Hartley at the school today as per my email from Clara, but I still have time to dash into work to check on a few emails. I can do them on my laptop at home, but I also like to check that everything has been cleaned up properly from the wedding the day before. Control freak problems.

I'm surprised when I see Hugh already there, looking around for something.

'Oh, there you are,' he says when he spots me. As if I was due in today at all. It's not officially in my contract to work Mondays, but I suppose he knows me too well.

'Hey. I didn't know you were coming in today. Did we plan a meeting or something?'

Now that I'm closer, I see his face has turned stern, his

jaw locked.

'No,' he says through gritted teeth. 'I'm here to ask you why the fuck you decided to involve my wife in a ridiculous mission yesterday?'

Wow. Hugh has never sworn at me before. He's bloody furious and I have no idea why, apart from Flo obviously telling him about her funny turn. Way to rat me out, Flo.

'Oh. Yeah... the thing is - '

'The thing is that my wife is not even an employee here,' he interrupts. 'You involved her in a stressful situation, on a *Sunday*, without clearing it with me.'

God, he's gone into full on headmaster mode. He's never been like this. I'm always made to feel more like a partner here than an employee. It's half the reason I work so hard. But when he speaks to me like this, I just want to headbutt him.

'Sorry, Hugh, but since when did I have to clear with you, me speaking with my best friend?' I ask sarcastically.

'When that talking involves her rushing around and making herself ill.'

I lean on one hip, attempting to show some defiance. 'Look, I agree. I didn't mean for her to get so tired she ended up nearly passing out on me.'

'Passing out?' he repeats, his eyes nearly bulging out of their sockets. 'What the fuck are you talking about?'

Wait... She didn't tell him? Way to go, Flo. Everyone

knows if you play down a situation you must let the other person know in case they're pulled on it. This is just like that time in PE when she'd told the teacher I'd vomited and then I went back in complaining of a sore ankle.

'Err... did I say passing out? She never *actually* passed out. Just got, you know, a bit tired. It's no big deal.'

'No big deal?' he roars, pushing himself off the wall and invading my space. 'You have no fucking idea, Nadine.'

Okay, now he's scaring me. Why the hell is he losing his rag so much? I've never seen him lose his composure like this.

'I obviously don't. What the hell am I missing here?'

'Nothing,' he barks, looking away from me. 'I just don't appreciate my wife being used to the point of exhaustion. She already has enough on as it is.'

'Why? What are you keeping from me?' Then it dawns on me. Flo's ill. That's why he's being overprotective and why she had her funny turn yesterday. Oh my God.

'Wait, is Flo ill?'

He turns away from me. 'She's fine.'

Why don't I believe him?

'Just stop dragging her around on your crazy pursuits. Next time the bride fucks up her dress just let her bridesmaids deal with it. Don't get so involved.'

'Fuck you, Hugh.' Ha ha, I didn't realise that rhymed. 'Until you tell me what the fuck is going on, don't expect me to be a mind reader. You can tell Flo from me, that if she still wants a best friend I'm here, but I won't be asking her husband's permission to speak to her.'

I grab my bag and storm out of there as dramatically as I can. It's just a shame the old creaky door doesn't slam and has to be closed a certain way for the latch to click.

My breath is coming in short pants, my heart beating erratically. I can't believe the fucking cheek of him. Here I am, fucking employee of the year and this prick is telling me off like I'm still in school. I'll be calling Flo and telling her what an arse her husband is, something you can only do when you've lived next door to your bestie all your life.

By the time I arrive at the school, I've just about calmed down. I can't believe I got talked into this. I really need to learn to say no, but if I'm honest with myself, I'm strangely looking forward to going back to a school environment.

After signing in at reception, I follow the directions to the main school hall. I push the door open, the mixed smell of bare feet and hot cheese assaulting my nostrils. There's a crowd of teenagers on the stage milling around, reading aloud from pieces of paper. I'm assuming it's a script. Jesus, I've forgotten how loud everything is. I'm so used to working in my own little bubble.

'Nadine.'

I jump from the sound of Hartley's deep voice behind me. I spin around to find him staring at me, his forest green eyes dancing in amusement. He has his arms crossed over his chest, his biceps bulging over in his tight shirt/jumper combo. Whoever thought a jumper could be so sexy?

'You scared me,' I admit, my voice high and jumpy.

He's just so large and manly. He must have modelled when he was younger, just got into teaching because he became too old for it.

'Thanks so much for this. I really appreciate it.'

'It's fine,' I quickly dismiss his comment, avoiding eye contact. Whenever I meet his gaze, I feel myself redden like a giggly teenager. It's a mortifying feeling. 'So where do you want me?'

His eyes lighten with mischief. God, did that sound whorish? Like I'm offering to sprawl myself out like a starfish for him?

'If you could help out with costumes that would be great.'

'No probs,' I nod eagerly. Far too eagerly. Calm down Nadine, you look like a nodding Churchill dog.

I busy myself by going towards the stage. Where are the costumes? Oh God, I really should have asked him that. I look back but he's halfway through rehearsing a scene with the kids. I can't interrupt that. Damn.

I look around to try to spot any kind of material. Well this is awkward.

'Are you okay?' a girl with long blonde hair asks me. She's got huge brown eyes that seem to take up most of her face. She's like a human version of Bambi.

'Um... I'm supposed to help with the costumes?'

'Ah, you'll need to go to the prop room then.' She starts walking. 'Follow me.'

Oh, thank God. A friendly and efficient teenager. I didn't think they existed anymore.

I follow her behind the stage and down some steps. It seems the prop room is under the stage. She opens the door to reveal a dimly lit room with crap everywhere. Wow, this place is beyond unorganised. It's giving me anxiety just looking at it.

'Wow,' I blurt out, without thinking.

'Yeah, it's a bit of a mess,' she admits with a grimace.

'Uh-huh.' I pick up an outfit just lying on the floor. 'What exactly does he want me to do with all this?'

She shrugs. 'Sorry, no idea. Good luck!'

Two hours later and I'm almost finished sorting the room. Without knowing what to do I thought I'd stick with what I'm good at, organising. So, I've sorted through everything and have a pile of outfits that need mending, some that need washing, and the ones in good order are now hung up in order of theme. I'm onto props now. I really wish I'd brought my label maker.

'Hey.'

I look up to see Hartley watching me, leaning against the doorframe. His shoulders take up most of the door.

'Hi,' I say shyly. 'Look, I wasn't sure what you wanted me to do, so I've just been organising what I can see.'

He checks over my piles. 'Well, that's more than Heather ever did. Don't worry, I kind of just threw you in the deep end.' He walks in, assessing the hung-up costumes.

'It's fine,' I shrug, looking at the floor. Why is it he makes me so edgy? It's taking a lot of effort to stop my jaw from chattering.

The door suddenly slams shut. I frown at him. 'I didn't feel a draft.'

He pouts. 'Me either.' He walks over to the door and tries the handle. 'It's stuck.' He puts his ear to the door. 'I hear giggling.' He bangs on it. 'Alright you lot, a joke's a joke, let us out now.'

More squealing giggles, this time loud enough for me to hear. Oh my God. They've locked us in.

'I mean it. Detention for everyone unless you let me out right this instant.'

'Sorry, Sir,' a boy laughs. 'But we're off for a bit of lunch.'

'I mean it, Marley!' he shouts furiously. 'Open up. NOW.'

Their giggles fade out until all we can hear is an eerie silence.

'Are they serious?' I ask in alarm. 'We can't really be stuck here, can we?' I look around at the tiny room barely big enough for five people.

There must be an emergency exit in case of a fire.

He sighs, as if exhausted. 'I'm afraid so. There's no other way out.'

My heart starts racing. Bit of a fire hazard isn't it?

The thought of not being able to get out claws at my throat. I start kicking the door, working up a sweat.

'Let me out!' I scream. 'Let me out!'

My chest tightens, and it's suddenly hard for me to breathe. I'm running out of air down here. God, am I dying? I fold myself down onto the floor, unable to move myself to a seat. A feeling of utter despair comes over me as if a physical dark cloud has descended.

'Nadine. Are you okay?' I hear Hartley ask as if in the distance. I can't move. I can't look at him to reassure him. I'm too busy dying.

My heart beats so fast and erratically I'm expecting it to explode out of my chest. I clutch it, hoping he'll realise I'm clearly having a heart attack and call an ambulance. Not that they'll be able to get us out. God, I'll have died by then. I knew I should have written a will while I had the chance. Not that I have much to my name, but there has to be some kind of cat charity I could leave my savings to, right?

I can't breathe. Why can't I breathe?

Hartley is suddenly in my face, squatting down next to me.

'Nadine, you're having a panic attack,' he explains

calmly.

Panic attack? I've never had a panic attack before and I'm pretty sure they don't feel like this. This is a real physical thing I'm feeling. Not just some freak out.

'I need you to breathe,' he commands calmly, locking eyes with me.

I frown. Can he not see that I'm trying to breathe dammit!

'You are my sunshine,' he starts singing. Why the hell is he singing right now? *'My only sunshine.'*

This is the song I used to sing to Belle when I was pregnant. No, don't think of that. That's only going to make me more upset. Instead I force myself to look into his strange coloured eyes and try to concentrate on how I'd describe the colour. I'm going to say they look more hazel today.

'You make me happy, when skies are grey.' My heart starts to slow down ever so slowly. *'You'll never know dear, how much I love you.'*

Belle will never know how much I love her. The despair squeezes at my chest.

He tucks a bit of my hair behind my ear. *'So please don't take my sunshine away.'*

She was taken away from me. A traitorous girly tear escapes out of my left eye. He wipes it away with his giant thumb before taking my hand and encouraging me to breathe slowly in and out. With every breath the oxygen slows down my erratic heart, my body heat returning close to normal.

Except now I don't know where to look. I just had a panic attack. I can't believe it. How mortifying to have done it in front of Hartley, a new client. A new client who's still staring at me intently.

'Well I'm glad I only ever taught five-year-olds. Teenagers are scary.'

He snorts a laugh. 'You're telling me. This lot drive me mad most days. Especially with me teaching drama. They think they can say whatever they want.'

I get up off the floor with his help and sit down on the old bench.

'I can't believe that just happened.' I cover my face with my hands, flustered.

He takes my hands and pulls them down, a kind smile gracing his lips. 'Don't be embarrassed. Was that the first one you've ever had?'

I nod.

'I take it you're claustrophobic?'

'Not really.' I think about it for a second.

Actually, I had something extremely similar after Belle. But only that one time and it was bloody understandable. Not that I can tell him that.

'I mean, I don't like the idea of not being able to get out from somewhere. Once, I had a cousin who used to lock me in a cupboard whenever the adults weren't around. I suppose it's scarred me.' I force a laugh to try to lighten the mood. 'How come you knew what it was?'

He was so calm.

'My mum used to suffer from them. I sang her that song. It probably sounded a bit random, but it worked for her.'

'And for me apparently.' I stand up onto shaky legs, eager to change the subject. 'Well, you might as well tell me what you want me to do. Looks like we're going to be in here for a while.'

'Sorry.' He slumps down next to me. 'I shouldn't have got you involved at all. I'd have never asked you to do something like this. It's so far away from your job description it's ridiculous, but Clara will do anything to get me more time.'

'That's nice of her.'

He snorts. 'No, it's time off so I'm more available for her every beck and call.'

'Oh.' I grimace. 'I'm not used to hearing that from happy fiancé's.'

He raises his eyes heavenwards. 'Yeah, well you don't know my fiancée very well yet.'

'Is... everything okay between you two?' I ask carefully, unable to stop myself.

He sighs again. 'Yeah. We're... fine.'

Hmm, why don't I believe him?

The door swings open, breaking us from the

awkwardness.

'Sorry, Sir,' the Bambi girl that helped me earlier says. 'I snuck back as soon as I could.'

'Thanks, Anna,' he smiles. So, Anna's her name.

We go to follow her out when I pull him back by his arm. 'Sorry for just losing my shit like that. It must have been cabin fever or something. You won't tell anyone, will you?'

The last thing I need is for it to get back to Hugh.

'Of course not. Your secret's safe with me.'

Tuesday 9th January

The girls and I have decided to go out tonight. Kelly has Wednesday's off work, so we always get talked into cheap drink Tuesday. It's supposed to just be for students, but we take full advantage of it. I'm lucky enough that I can make sure I don't schedule any important meetings on a Wednesday. Not that I tell Hugh that.

I meet them at a Wetherspoons in town, the girls having already taken advantage of the two-for-one cocktails. I get myself one and settle down for our weekly gossip.

'So, what I want to know,' Florence says leaning in eagerly over the mayhem of uni students, 'is what is going on between Mia and Troy?'

Mia rolls her eyes, but her cheeks flush scarlet.

'You're blushing.' Kelly says, bashing shoulders with Mia. 'Come on. Spill.'

'There's nothing going on,' she protests, trying desperately to hide her smile. 'We're just friends.'

'Friends my arse,' I scoff. 'You must be having sex at the very least.'

'We're not,' she insists, her heavily black eye-lined eyes glaring back at me. 'Neither of us are ready for a relationship, so we're just friends.'

'Friends that fuck?' Flo asks, grinning from ear to ear.

'No! Jesus. You guys. We're just good mates. We've agreed that we'd hate to sleep with each other and ruin what we have right now. So instead we're just the best of friends.'

'Wait,' Flo says with a scowl. 'Are you serious? You really are just mates?'

'Yes. Jesus, it's not my fault all you dirty bitches assume I'm getting serviced by him.'

'Serviced?' I crease over laughing.

'But seriously,' Kelly says, her eyes creased in confusion. 'If you're best mates and there's a sexual attraction there, then why not just become a couple?'

'Because we don't want that,' she explains with an eye roll. 'We're not ready to settle down. We both want to play the field a bit.'

'So, what you're saying,' I interrupt, 'is that you both know you're perfect for one another; you just plan to have a good play around before settling down together.'

'Well, we haven't actually said that to each other,' she admits, twisting her hands in her lap. 'But yeah, kind of, I suppose.'

We all burst out laughing.

Florence raises her cocktail. 'Well, here's to Mia and Troy and their future wedding.'

We all cheer to that. All apart from Mia.

Four hours later and I'm a little bit shit-faced. Those Prosecco cocktails from the club we've moved onto were a bit of a mistake, but my God, do they taste delicious. I excuse myself and queue up with uni students for the toilet.

I go in, do my business and then leave. I'm almost at the sink when I feel a fart slip out. Only... the feeling down my leg tells me it wasn't just a fart. Shit! Literally.

Shoving the girl headed for my toilet cubicle out of the way, I run in, locking the door behind me. I take down my playsuit and find to my absolute horror that I've shit my pants. I'm thirty-two years old and I've just shit my pants. What the fuck!

Its liquid diarrhoea and its run all down my legs. How the hell could this have happened? I haven't eaten anything dodgy. Well, I suppose we did have those kebabs on the way here, but still. You think you're safe with a drunken kebab, then the next thing you know you're shitting yourself.

I get toilet tissue and quickly clean myself up the best I can. I take off my knickers and throw them away in the sanitary bin, cursing myself that I wore my favourite ones. The worst thing is that my jumpsuit is the same material as a swimming costume, so it seems to have absorbed some of it.

Ugh, I'm gonna have to go straight home. I get my phone out and order an Uber. Next, I text the girls and tell them there's been an emergency and that I'm going straight home. I watch as my Uber comes around the corner. I scrub my hands as best as I can, hoping to God I don't stink of shit.

I run out front and spot the car listed. I go to the driver window, wanting to double check it's an Uber, when I nearly jump out of my skin. Why the hell is Hartley here?

'Hartley?'

'Oh, Nadine.' His cheeks redden. 'I didn't realise it was you I was collecting.'

'Wait, are you telling me you're an Uber driver?'

He nods, pressing his lips together. 'Three evenings a week. Trying to make a bit of extra money for our honeymoon. I don't earn the same as Clara.'

'I doubt anyone does,' I blurt out in my drunken stupor.

I open the back seat, but then realise I don't want to put my shitty arse on his car seats. What if it seeps into the seat and smells for days, even weeks later? I could be his last pick up of the night. He'll know it was me. God, I'd never be able to look at him again.

I only have one option. I jump in, face first so my arse doesn't touch the seats.

'Are you okay there?' he asks, looking back at me with amusement in his eyes.

'Yeah, I'm just feeling sleepy,' I say pretending to be more drunk than I am.

He raises his eyebrows, nodding, clearly completely unconvinced. 'Right... Whatever you say. Just the address you put into the app, right?'

'Yep, that's it.'

God, I must look insane. I lift my head up with my hand, to try to look like I'm more relaxed.

He rolls the window down. Can he smell me?

'God, I hate the smell of manure around here,' he says, as if to himself.

Oh God. He can. I roll down my window too. 'Yeah, terrible.'

'So, good night, was it?' he asks, glancing back at me in his rearview mirror.

'Yeah. Had a few too many I think,' I admit on a giggle. *You know, ended up shitting myself. The usual Tuesday night shenanigans.*

'Well, then it sounds like a great night. Bit of a random night to go out though isn't it?'

'Two-for-one Tuesday,' I explain.

'Ah,' he nods. 'Girl after my own heart.'

He pulls up outside my parents' house. 'This is me. Thanks.'

He turns around to face me. 'No probs. Listen...' he licks his lips, as if nervous. 'You won't mention this to Clara, will you?'

I frown, my drunk mind catching up slowly. 'Wait, your fiancée doesn't know about your extra job? Isn't that kind of weird?'

He sighs. 'Look, it's just easier. If I say I'm doing it for extra money, she'll just lay on the pressure to go and work for her dad.'

I shrug. 'Okay.'

'Look, I don't need your judgement, okay?' he snaps, his jovial mood gone.

'Fine,' I snort, sliding out backwards from the car. 'Bye!'

I slam the car of the door far harder than I ought to. But I don't care. Right now, I'm angry and I just want a shower.

Chapter 4

Thursday 11th January

I'm still embarrassed two days later when I hand over the sheets to both Clara and Hartley at their food tasting. I can't look Hartley in the eye. Aside from him possibly being suspicious of me shitting myself, I was rude to him. I'm never normally drunk around clients, but then I suppose it's not my fault he's also a part-time Uber driver. I was off duty and allowed to let my hair down, surely?

'These are so you can score your meals and write down any comments or suggestions you have. You'd be surprised how overwhelming it can be.' I smile professionally.

'We are just trying food, right?' Hartley asks, an amused smirk appearing.

I glare back at him before quickly covering it with a

professional smile. 'Like I say, you'd be surprised.' What a dick.

'Yes, Ley,' Clara whines. 'This is important.'

She calls him Ley? Ugh, why on earth would you shorten a gorgeous name like Hartley to Ley? Monster.

She flicks her hair over her shoulder. 'I for one am not going to serve a sub-standard meal to my guests.'

God, she's annoying.

'I can assure you that what you're about to try will be delicious. All our meat and vegetables are sourced locally, and our chef has been with us over a year. He actually used to own the pub before we took over and was here for twelve years.'

'So, he knows the place,' Clara smiles with an understanding nod.

'Yep. He definitely knows his way around the kitchen.' God, I sound cheesy sometimes.

Florence comes walking out from the back dressed in her black trousers and a white shirt I asked her to wear. Thank God. My usual waitress let me down, so I called her in last minute. I wasn't sure if she was going to show, what with Hugh being so overbearingly overprotective, but I saw her walking round the back at the same time as Clara and Hartley arrived.

'Ah, and here is our waitress for the day, Florence.'

'Hi,' she waves, the smile not meeting her eyes.

Now I look closer at her she looks a bit grey. There are

dark rings around her eyes too. I need to corner her as soon as this is over. Something's going on. With the way Hugh reacted the other day I wouldn't be surprised if there was trouble in their marriage.

'Hi, Florence,' Clara says, standing up to air-kiss her. Hartley nods a hello.

'They're ready for the starter course, when you are, Flo,' I say, then smile while asking with my eyes if she's okay.

She nods discreetly. 'Of course. Coming right up.' She disappears into the kitchen, an unsettling silence descending over us.

I'm just about to ask how their week was when the front door bangs open and Emily, the sixty-year-old cleaner, comes in carrying her vacuum.

'Oh, hi, Emily,' I smile, standing up. *What the hell is she doing here?* 'I thought I cancelled you this morning. We're doing a tasting, you see.'

'Oh, right,' she says, her eyes falling in disappointment. Half of me thinks she just likes getting out of the house. Since her husband retired, she'll find any excuse to be out and about.

I feel bad letting her down like this. She doesn't mean any harm.

'Or... you could clean as long as you do it quietly? No vacuuming.'

'Yes.' She grins broadly, warming my heart. 'Sounds

good.'

I look back to Clara. 'Emily here has been cleaning this pub for the last twenty years.'

'Really?' Clara says, looking at her with her nose scrunched up, as if she's a bit of dirt on her shoe. She was probably brought up to treat cleaners as staff. Stuck up cow.

'Yep,' Emily nods, completely oblivious to her disdain. 'Oh, the things I've seen over the years in this place.'

Oh God, I always forget how unpredictable she can be. We don't want her telling them about all the vomit she's scooped up over the years.

'Thank you, Emily,' I say with a tight smile, hoping she'll get the hint to leave.

'Especially over this last year,' she continues. 'Since the wedding business I've found all sorts. Used condoms are the worst. You'd think the dirty beggars would want to dispose of them after, but they never do.'

'Yes, *thank you,* Emily!' I almost shout. 'We'd love to chat but we're *very* busy tasting.'

'Oh,' she says, looking crestfallen. 'Okay. I know where I'm not wanted.' She flounces off to the other end of the bar with a humph. Jesus. I didn't mean to upset the bitch.

Florence comes out of the door holding two trays. Now her face looks kind of green.

'You have a few options when it comes to the starter. We have our winter vegetable soup.' Florence places the tray down in front of them containing the little pot with a fresh baked roll on the side. 'The mozzarella salad. Or the pate.'

'Ugh.' We all turn to look at Florence, who I'm guessing made the noise. She covers her mouth quickly. 'Excuse me.' She runs off towards the toilet.

I grimace. 'Sorry about that.'

It's then that the sound of violent vomiting echoes around the room from the bathroom. The poor cow is really going for it. I frown back at them.

Clara puts her fork down pointedly.

'Maybe I'll put on a bit of background music?' I suggest, already running behind the bar and looking at the stereo system. I press play, glad for the music immediately blasting out loudly, covering the vomiting noise.

Only then I notice the woman singing the lyrics. It's *My Neck, My Back* by *Khia*. She starts singing about how she wants her man to lick and suck her pussy and then her crack. Dear God! What kind of wedding reception did we host if this is the last song played?

I look over to find Hartley has burst out laughing and is currently holding his sides from chuckling so hard. Clara looks very unamused, her eyebrows raised as if expecting an explanation.

'Sorry.' I shout, trying to pause it. But the fucker won't pause. Right, I'll turn it off instead. I press the stop button but that's sticking and doesn't seem to work either. Why is this happening to me?

I finally find the power cord and yank the whole thing out of the plug, but in the process also knock the system onto the floor. Oops.

'Sorry about that.' I say, all in a fluster, deciding to just style it out. I can worry about the replacement stereo later.

Florence's vomiting echoes back around the room. God, how can the poor cow still be going at it?

'Shall we perhaps move onto the mains?' I ask, getting up and collecting the uneaten tray of food. I know I'm going to have to do it myself. There's no way Flo's in any fit state.

I rush into the kitchen and grab the tray containing two roast dinners under the hot lamp.

'Where's Flo?' Marty, the chef, asks.

'Hungover,' I answer with an eye roll. Except now I realise; she must be pregnant.

I can't believe I haven't thought of it until now. She's been tired, nearly passed out, and now she's sick? That would also explain why Hugh went mad at me. I'm such an idiot. But then... she was drinking cocktails on Tuesday. Surely, she wouldn't risk that? Thinking about it she insisted on buying. I bet hers were virgin cocktails and she pretended to be drunk.

I walk out, struggling to hold the heavy plates. God, how do the waitresses do this? It's hard bloody work just holding two, and I'm always snapping at them to go faster. They must hate me. No wonder my nickname is snow queen.

I take a second to compose myself before walking back down the corridor towards Clara and Hartley. I'm nearly at the table when Florence comes barrelling out of the bathroom, crashing right into me.

'Flo!' I shout, as I try but fail to swerve right and miss her. I end up mis-stepping and come crashing down onto the floor, my face landing in a roast dinner. I pull my face up from it and wipe the mashed potato from my nose, while gravy drips down my cheeks.

'I'm so sorry.' Florence exclaims, trying to pull me up. I look over to see Clara looking on in revulsion.

Strong hands are suddenly underneath my arms and I'm hoisted up to standing so quick I get a head rush. I steady myself against Hartley's chest, shocked he's rushed to my rescue.

'Are you okay?' he asks, attempting to wipe my face with his napkin. His worried forest-green eyes check over me, as if I'm made of glass.

For a second, I forget how to talk completely.

'Yeah, I'm...' God. Mortified? Dying of embarrassment? Take your pick.

'I think maybe we should reschedule this?' he suggests. Is that a hint of amusement in the corners of his mouth? It better bloody not be. I'll kill him.

'Yes. I agree it would be best for us to reschedule.' I nod furiously, clinging onto the smallest hint of professionalism.

Jesus, first I have a panic attack in front of him, then smell of shit in the back of his car, and now I'm throwing gravy dinners over myself. What a great impression he must have of me: a clumsy, mentally instable, poo smelling woman.

They quickly leave, but not before Emily tells them how hard it is to get the smell of vomit out of a pub. *Fantastic.*

'Nadine.' I turn to see Florence looking a lot paler than a minute ago.

'Are you okay?'

I've barely finished the question before she vomits on my shoes. Just when you think it can't get any worse...

'I'm not okay,' she utters, wiping her mouth. 'I'm pregnant.'

'I knew it!'

I wait for the expected feelings of jealousy to overtake me. The same feelings I've felt whenever I've been invited to a baby shower, christening, or first birthday party. The crushing guilt that I couldn't keep my baby. But it never comes. Instead a euphoria overtakes me, causing noticeable goosepimples on my arms.

'Flo, I'm so happy for you.' I fling her into my arms, not caring if she vomits down my back.

She pulls away to look up at me, frowning. 'Are you really?'

'Yes! Of course, I am. Don't let what happened with me ruin what's happening with you. I'm so happy for you guys.'

She finds a seat and sits down. 'Thanks. But... ugh, I'm so ill. I'm not even sure if I'm going to make it to Lydia's wedding.'

I remember those days well. It's insane to think I kind of miss it in a way. It was my body's way of showing me I was still pregnant.

'My sister's wedding should be the last thing on your mind. Like she'd even notice. You know how bridezilla she's become. I'll drive you home and put you back to bed.'

She smiles weakly back at me. 'Thank you.'

'So, I take it this is why Hugh went so mental at me for involving you in the bloody bride disaster the other day?'

Her eyes widen. 'He did not go mad at you. Did he?' Her shoulders droop, as if she already knows the answer.

'It's fine. I get it. He's being protective because you're carrying his baby.' I smile whenever I think of a mini Florence and Hugh.

'It's not just that.' She sighs, putting her head in her hands. 'He previously lost a baby with Felicity.'

'Felicity? That whore that tried to stop you getting married?'

She snorts a laugh. 'Yeah, that's the one.'

I feel a new compassion for her. She may be a bitch but losing a baby changes you. Makes you hard, jaded. A

bitch, even.

'Well, just because it happened with her doesn't mean it'll happen to you,' I offer weakly. I mean, really, who the hell am I to tell her to stay positive? I'm proof that anything can bloody happen. It's beyond your control.

'I know,' she nods. 'But until I've had my twelve-week scan, I won't relax. Neither will Hugh. They were ten weeks gone when they miscarried before.'

'How many weeks are you?' I can't help but ask.

'I'm only seven weeks. It's seriously early days.'

I take her hand and squeeze it tight. 'It's going to work out for you. I know it.'

Her eyes fill with tears. 'How do you? After what happened to you, how can you be positive about anything?'

I smile back sadly. 'You're not me, Flo. You're going to be fine.'

'How can you say that?' she demands, a tear escaping, trailing down her cheek. 'I've only had this baby inside me a couple of weeks and already the fear of losing it has my heart breaking. I just... I don't know how you survived it, Nads. I really don't.'

Sometimes I don't either. But life goes on regardless and sooner or later you have to start going back through the motions of living.

'Because I was too much of a pussy to take my own life,' I joke.

She narrows her eyes at me. 'You were suicidal?' she

shrieks in disbelief. 'You never told me that.'

Oh Jesus. I can't be telling her this stuff while she's in such a fragile state.

'Of course, I wasn't. Just joking.' She blinks rapidly, as if not believing me. 'Look, I got on with things because I had no other choice. Now, let's take your wedding ring off and use my necklace to see if it's a boy or a girl.'

She laughs. 'You know that's a load of crap.'

'Hey! Maybe we need some superstitious silliness right now to take your mind off the seriousness.'

She bursts into heavy tears. 'Nadine, I bloody love you sometimes.'

I allow her to hug me tight as she sobs on my shoulder. I say a silent prayer to a God I no longer believe in. Please God, if you're real, don't let it happen to Florence. Not her.

Thursday 11th January

I'm back at the high school this evening helping out these little brats they call kids. It's getting easier though. I wonder whether Hartley has had a word with them. That or I'm getting so used to my sister Lydia's enraged phone calls every time something with her wedding goes askew that I'm becoming more tolerant in general.

I've helped small pairs of kids practice their lines of Romeo and Juliet and I'm just clearing up the outfits for the day when Anna, the sweet Bambi-eyed girl that let us out of here yesterday, comes in, tears streaming down her face.

'Hey, what's up?' I ask, immediately going to her and pulling her into an awkward side hug.

'Ugh, everything! I've fucked everything up. I'm useless,' she wails, wiping her eyes with the back of her hand.

God, I forgot how everything is the end of the world when you're a teenager.

'Ssh, don't be silly.' I start to subconsciously rock her like you would a baby. 'It might feel awful now, but I promise you there's nothing that can't be fixed.'

'Really?' she asks sarcastically, pulling back and wiping her nose with the back of her hand. 'I don't see how you can fix a baby away. Last time I checked that was called an abortion.'

What the fuck?

'Whoa! Wait, are you telling me you're *pregnant?*'

She sniffs, her eyes falling to the floor. 'Yeah.' Her huge brown eyes find mine again, filled with trepidation. 'Now try to tell me how everything will be okay.'

'Oh, Anna.'

If I would have guessed on anyone being pregnant it would have been that slut Chelsea with the neon pink bra, not sweet Anna.

'The school will expel me when they find out, and then I won't be able to finish taking my GCSE's. I'll probably end up working full time in New Look or something.' She gulps, more tears welling in her eyes.

My heart sinks for her. Why does it always happen to the nice kids? I try to think of something to cheer her up.

'No. I'm going to help you,' I announce with a determined nod. 'You can take your GCSE's at college if the school finds out, but until then you need to hide this as best you can. Keep your head down and study like mad.'

She smiles back gratefully. 'Thanks, Nadine.' She sniffs. 'You're so nice. I wish my mum was as understanding as you.'

'Oh, I'm sure your mum loves you.' I scribble down my number for her. 'Here, take this and call me anytime you want to chat.'

She smiles and turns to walk out of the door. She pauses just before leaving and turns around. 'Nadine?'

'Yeah?'

'You never asked me if I wanted an abortion. What made you assume I wanted to keep it?'

God, she's right. That's terrible of me, to just assume.

'Oh, I'm sorry. I didn't think. I just...' I think of my Belle. 'Well, I suppose I just see any baby as a miracle, regardless of the crummy situation.'

She smiles brightly. 'Thank you.' She walks out, her shoulders no longer as drooped as before. I'm glad I've given her some hope. 'Oh, hi, Sir,' I hear her say.

Oh no, Hartley. Did he hear anything?

He enters the room and I immediately know he heard from his tense jaw and bunched eyebrows.

'Hey,' he smiles uneasily.

'How much did you hear?' I ask, too weary to beat around the bush. It's been a long day.

He sits down on the bench and rests his head in his hands. 'She's pregnant?' He phrases it like a question, but it's clear he already knows.

I nod.

He looks devastated. Clearly this is more than the normal teacher/student relationship. Shit... you don't think he's the father? Oh my God!

'You're not the father, are you?' I ask with a gasp.

His mouth drops to the floor. 'Are you fucking serious?'

'Well... I was,' I admit, suddenly feeling stupid.

'Jesus! I haven't started to shag my students. Or anyone other than Clara for that matter,' he confirms with a condemning shake of his head.

Well, thank God for that. All respect for him was quickly going down the toilet. I was already wondering whether I'd have to go to the police, as well as to see Clara, and the headteacher.

'Okay, I'm sorry. It's just that you look so pale and worried.'

I'm really not used to teachers caring so much about their students. I remember telling Mr Conlon about my concerns of Maddie Charston being bullied for the strawberry birthmark on her forehead and he couldn't have given less of a shit. Poor Maddie. It was Max Factor that sorted her out in the end.

'Of course, I'm fucking worried. She's my student and now she's knocked up.'

'Sssh!' I hiss, jumping up to close the door. 'You don't want this getting out.'

He sighs heavily, swiping his hand through his hair. 'Why didn't you persuade her to consider an abortion? What was with the *"all babies are miracles"* crap?'

Just thinking of Belle again has me gasping for breath. I falter, staggering backwards slightly, hitting my back against the door.

'Nadine, are you okay?' He jumps up and is in front of me within a second. 'You look like you're about to faint. Are you having another panic attack?' He holds my upper arms as if to steady me.

At just this tiny act of comfort, I feel the unshed tears brimming at my eyes. All of the tears I hold in every day since it happened. I want nothing more than to collapse in his arms, crush my face into his warm chest and sob my heart out. Ask him to hold me, stroke my hair, tell me everything will be alright. But I can't. I know that. I barely know this man. And what I do know is that he's due to marry someone else.

I take a deep breath. 'I'm fine,' I assure him, my voice

shaky and completely unbelievable.

His thumb gently lifts my chin. 'Hey, I'm sorry if what I said upset you. I can be a heartless bastard sometimes.'

'It didn't,' I say hastily, pushing his hand away. I don't want to look him in the eye when I lie to him. 'Sorry, I'm just being weird and emotional. I must be due on or something.'

He frowns. Jesus, why on God's holy earth did I think it acceptable to tell him I'm due on my period? I'm not even due for another few weeks. Now he's going to be thinking of me bleeding. Ugh, poor bastard will probably need to have therapy.

His eyes bore into me until I'm forced to look at him.

'Nadine, I think you've got a massive heart, that's all.'

I sniff and shake my head.

'I mean it. I heard what you said to Anna. Anyone else would have been horrified at the idea of a pregnant teenager, but you were so kind to her. You gave her hope.'

'She does have hope,' I say defiantly, already feeling strangely overprotective of her. 'Even if the school finds out, she can still do her GCSE's at college.'

He scoffs. 'And you think she'll be able to do that while pregnant? Carry on her education with a baby around?'

I cross my arms over my chest. 'All I know is that if she wants that baby, everything else is just background noise.'

He looks at me, a strange expression on his face. 'You're very odd, you know that?'

I snort a bitchy laugh. 'Just because I actually like kids, unlike your fiancée.'

He glares back at me. 'Hey! That's not fair.'

'Why isn't it?' I snap. 'She said so herself. She doesn't want kids. Don't you want them?'

I know I shouldn't have asked such a personal question, but it's pretty clear that this isn't the normal client/planner relationship.

'Of course, I do,' he grumbles, turning to comb his hair through with his hand. 'It's not that simple.'

'Really? Because it sounds to me like you don't want to face up to the realities of your future marriage.'

His face scrunches up, his forest-green eyes flashing with animosity towards me. 'Fuck you, Nadine. You know nothing.'

He stands, turns, and storms out of the room, slamming the door shut behind him.

Oops.

Chapter 5

'Where the hell is he?' Clara demands, looking at her Cartier watch with a pout.

I'm not sure if she's expecting me to answer her or if she just wants to voice her rage.

Hartley's ten minutes late for his own engagement photoshoot being held here at The Duck and Goose. It makes me wonder if he's given what I said some thought. If he's halfway to New Zealand by now, I couldn't blame him. Not wanting to marry this prissy thing.

'He knows what time the appointment was. God, I hope he's not been held up by another bloody student of his. I swear, they're so clingy.'

She's a heartless cow.

'Hi, sorry, sorry!' Hartley says, rushing in looking

frazzled. He avoids my gaze and instead pecks a chaste kiss on Clara's cheek.

Not changed his mind then. Quite willing to get married to someone who doesn't want the same things as him. I don't know why I even care. Maybe because it's making a complete mockery of the whole institution of marriage? Something I care deeply about.

'Ready to get this show on the road?' the photographer asks, fiddling with his camera lens. 'I'd like you over here, with the trees as a backdrop.'

'Well, are we?' Clara demands to Hartley, hand on her hip like a tea pot handle.

He rolls his eyes. 'Yes. I'm here now.'

He looks over to me, his cheeks slightly pink. Is he embarrassed that he's still going ahead with this sham after admitting to me that they want different things? He bloody should be.

Look at him, hugging her from behind for the photographer. Gazing down at her adoringly. Can love really be that blind that you ignore your future together?

Ugh, I can't watch. I go inside and attempt to busy myself with some paperwork. It's hard though when you're as efficient as me. I have to stay until the shoot is finished so I decide to make them both a frothy hot chocolate. It's still freezing out. Most people are looking forward to spring, but I love the cosiness of winter. There's nothing better than relaxing in front of the fire with a warm mug of hot chocolate.

I'm just bringing them out, pleased with my artwork of chocolate shavings and mini marshmallows when I almost walk into Hartley striding back into the pub.

'Whoa!' we both say at the same time, barely missing bumping into each other.

I steady the mugs so that only a small bit drips down the sides.

'Sorry,' he grimaces. 'I didn't mean to startle you.'

I find I can't look him in the eye. What is wrong with me? I can't help but feel embarrassed that I spoke so freely last night. I must remember that he's a client.

'Oh, that's fine. I was just bringing you and Clara a hot chocolate.'

He smiles, his face lit up at the idea. Wow, he must really love hot chocolate.

'She's gone back to work. But I'll have it.' He carefully takes a mug from me. 'I love hot chocolate.'

'Very manly of you,' I joke, sitting down at a table so I can sip the leftover one. My God, I make a good hot chocolate.

'Yep. Me man. Me like hot chocolate,' he jokes in a Tarzan voice, hitting his chest.

I smile and take another sip. Why is this awkward? You could cut the uneasy tension with a knife.

'Anyway, I was coming in here to ask if you're planning on coming back to the school tomorrow night to help out with the play?' His eyes portray the vulnerability in the question.

I'm surprised he's swallowing his pride and asking, with how it ended the other night.

I fiddle with the mug handle. 'Well, I wasn't sure you wanted me there anymore. You know, after you told me to go fuck myself.'

He sighs, looking down at the table. 'Of course, I do.'

I smile back, his eyes finding mine and holding them in place. It's like they're hypnotic.

'Besides, it's too late to find someone else now,' he grins, attempting to break the atmosphere.

I hit him on the arm. 'Cheeky bastard!'

'Come on. I'm sorry for what I said about Anna. I'd really like it if you were there. You're so bloody organised. Without you it'll probably go to shit.'

I smile smugly. 'Well, I am pretty awesome,' I agree with a nod. 'So... I'll think about it.'

'Think about it?' he asks, his eyes widened in disbelief.

He's obviously used to everyone doing whatever he asks of them. Sex God that he is.

'Yep. I'll think about it.' I take another sip, trying to act nonchalant. 'Is Clara coming to the play?'

'Yeah,' he nods. 'She's getting off work early for it.'

'That's nice of her,' I say sincerely.

He presses his lips into a fine line. 'There's no need to be sarcastic,' he snaps, squinting his eyes at me in disgust.

'I know you don't like her, but there's no need to take the piss.'

I gasp, shocked by his outburst and opinion of me. 'I wasn't taking the piss. I was seriously saying I'm glad she's supporting you.'

'What, because she can't be bothered to support me normally? Because she wants me to give it up and get a real job?'

'Hey,' I hold my hands up in surrender. 'You are literally going off on a tangent right now. I never said or meant anything like that.'

He sighs, running his hand through his tied up hair. 'I'm sorry, I'm just being sensitive. I'm worried it's all going to go to hell.'

'What, the play or the marriage?' I smirk. Okay, maybe I can see why he'd think I'm against his marriage. I'm hardly acting like a supportive wedding planner.

'The play,' he answers sternly fiddling with his watch. 'Why are you so down on my impending marriage?'

'I'm not! I'm a bloody wedding planner for God's sake.'

'Which has clearly made you jaded.' He raises his eyebrows as if wanting me to challenge him.

'The only jaded person here is you,' I insist, pointing an accusing finger at his chest. God, it's broad. No Nadine, for God's sake, concentrate.

He sighs, standing up, having cleared his hot chocolate. 'Whatever. I don't have time to argue about this.

Are you coming tomorrow or not?'

I stare back at him defiantly. 'Fine, I'll be there. Much like you, I don't break a promise. Regardless of how much I regret it.'

Saturday 13th January

I watch on anxiously as the bride ties the wedding rings to her dog Benny's collar. She insisted on her golden retriever being a part of the ceremony. Hugh made me take double our usual deposit in case it shits somewhere. I'm more worried about the dog behaving and making it through without trashing the place.

The bride is getting her make-up done while I assess the danger. She's clearly oblivious to all the potential damage this dog could cause.

'Would you be able to take him outside?' the bride asks me with a hopeful smile. 'He needs the toilet before the wedding.'

I stare back at her. Is she serious? She stares back at me expectantly. Okay, so she clearly is. Now I can add dog walker to my CV next to wedding planner/manager. God, my life is glamorous.

I take the lead with a forced smile. 'Of course.'

I lead Benny, the big bastard, out to the front and wait for him to make his move. He just stares back up at me as if waiting for instruction. I roll my eyes at him. Jesus, all that stuff about dogs being intelligent is clearly crap. I'm definitely a cat girl.

'Come on Benny, have a poo poo.'

Dear God, I can't believe I'm talking to a dog, telling him to have a poo poo. What has my life come to? But I don't think I can say the word shit around him. Almost like he's a child and will know I said a naughty word. Tell his mummy on me.

'Come on, Benny,' I say more cheerfully. 'You want to have your poo poo now and not in the middle of the ceremony.' He tilts his head to one side, his eyes narrowing, one ear cocking up. 'That's right, Benny. We don't want it to happen while mummy and daddy are getting married. Saying their vows,' I clarify, as if he'll understand if I explain it enough.

'Oh Jesus, I'm talking to a frigging dog.'

I get my phone out and start googling how to get a dog to poo. I start watching the first video that comes up. Some training woman giving the dog treats when it poos in the same spot. Well that's not what I want. I want it to poo *now*.

A loud gulp makes me turn towards Benny. Why does his face look weird? He hunches his shoulders over and starts retching, obviously trying to bring something up. Like he just ate... Oh my God. He wouldn't have... right?

I grab his collar, desperately searching round for the

ring bag. It's not there. Shit the fucking bed, it's not there. I search around in a last-ditch hope of finding it strewn on the floor. No such luck.

He's eaten it. The stupid bloody bastard has eaten the ring bag. The bride mustn't have secured it enough. Jesus, you'd think if you were tying your wedding rings to a stupid dog you'd do a bloody double knot. That's basic Brownie 101.

Well, what the hell am I going to do now?

She'll need it cut out. I can't go back to the bride and tell her I've allowed him to eat it while I supervised. You'd think I'd be able to handle a bloody dog. Of all the potential disasters I did not see this coming. I chastise myself.

Right. Think Nadine. Think.

How the hell am I going to get these rings out? I grab him by the collar while he's still attempting to retch it out. Maybe I can help him to get sick. Hmm, with humans we just stick our fingers down our throats. At least that's what my university flatmate, Hayley, used to do after a wild night out on the session.

I move my fingers cautiously into his mouth. Ugh, his mouth is all wet, warm, and gooey. He starts licking me. Of course, he does. This dog has the IQ of an onion.

'No, Benny. I'm trying to help you.'

I push my two fingers closer to his throat and don't stop until he starts retching again. A tiny bit of vomit jumps up and hits my hand.

'Eeew!' I scream, shaking my hand around. I find some grass and wipe it off as best I can. Dammit, where is my anti-bacterial lotion when I need it! I knew I should have put one in this coat.

He carries on retching, but nothing else is coming up. I straddle him and start massaging his stomach.

'Come on Benny boy. Get that bag up. You want your mummy and daddy to get married, don't you?' I encourage in what I'm hoping are soothing tones.

I look up to see a wedding guest walking past me. He gives me the strangest look. Yeah, yeah. I talk to dogs I'm straddled over. Lap it up, arsehole.

I grab some of the grass and offer it to him to eat. Cows eat grass, so dogs can too, right? Actually, don't they naturally eat plants and things when they're trying to bring stuff up? I'm sure I heard that from somewhere.

He doesn't take it though. Just turns his nose up at it as if I've offered him a shit sandwich. Ungrateful little fuck. Okay, I'm sweating now. This is going from disaster to disaster.

I need to speak to a vet. But the wedding is due to start in the next ten minutes. I can't make it to a vet and back in that time. I could call Flo, ask for her help? But then I remember the baby and the overprotective Hugh. No, I can't do that.

For a moment, I consider running up to the bride and asking for her help, but this is the last thing she needs. I'll

grab the maid of honour instead. I call her phone, thankfully having had the forethought to save it in my phone, and pray she answers.

'Hi, Nadine. Is everything okay?' she asks straightaway.

'No. I need you to discreetly come down to the front where I have Benny.'

'Oh, okay. I'll be two minutes.'

I carry on massaging Benny's stomach until she finally appears, carrying her floor length peach bridesmaid dress.

'What's up?' she asks before she's even stopped running. 'Is it Benny?'

'Yes, it's Benny,' I say through gritted teeth. 'He's eaten the rings.'

'Oh my God!' she shrieks, her eyes nearly bursting out of their sockets. 'What are we going to do?'

Well, she's working out to be a whole lot of help. Not.

'We need to get a vet. Do you know anyone in the wedding party that has experience with animals?' I ask desperately.

'Yes!' she says, jumping up at her excellent idea. 'I do. Wait here, I'll go get him.'

Thank God. There's a vet among the guests. Of course, there is. They're dog people. This is all going to be fine.

'Don't worry Benny. Help is coming.'

She's back a few minutes later with a tall man in his late thirties.

'What's the problem?' he asks me, looking at Benny. 'Shelby said something about the dog being sick.'

Oh great. Thanks Shelby. Making me explain it to him.

'The dog ate the wedding rings.' I don't have time to sugar coat it. 'I need them out of him *now*. Can you perform emergency surgery?'

He starts laughing.

'Sorry, but what part of this is funny, exactly?' I'm so pissed off I imagine launching myself at him and punching him repeatedly in his stupid face.

'Sorry,' he scoffs. 'It's just that there is no way I'm performing emergency surgery on a dog.'

'Why the hell not?' I demand, hand on hip. Does he not care about his friend's wedding day? Selfish bastard.

He snorts. 'Well first of all I'm only a veterinary nurse.'

A nurse? She's brought me a bloody veterinary nurse?

'And secondly, you can't just demand surgery on a perfectly healthy dog.'

'He's not healthy!' I shriek. 'He has a bloody bag of rings somewhere inside his intestines! Surely that's going to fuck his insides up?' I glare back at the bridesmaid. 'Well you guys have been no help. I'll have to drive him into town.'

'There's no point,' he says, shaking his head. 'No vet will operate on him. You're better off looking for new rings.'

New rings? Does he just think I have a couple of spare

wedding rings lying around? Some fucking jewellers from Hatton Garden on speed dial? Bloody idiot.

'But the wedding is due to start in three minutes!' Shelby shouts. 'We have no time for that!'

'Okay, calm down, Shelby,' I say in a calm, authoritative voice, attempting to shut her up.

It seems to calm her slightly. Okay, I need to think of a plan. Something to make sure this couple get married.

'You need to go around all of the guests and see if anyone has any spare rings that could fit and be appropriate to fill in.'

'Got it,' she nods. 'Wait, what are you going to do?'

Is she trying to imply I'm lazy? I will take that bitch down.

'I'm going to try to talk it out with Benny.'

She nods, while the nurse snorts a laugh. They both turn and head back.

I look down at Benny. I reach into my coat pocket and grab out my keys. There is one other option. I could do the surgery myself. Stab him in the gut and pull the rings out myself with my bare hands.

Shit the bed.

Did I really just think that? What the hell is wrong with me?

Have I really lost it so badly that I'm considering gutting a family dog just for a pair of stupid rings? I hand the dog over to the girl behind the bar, scared to be left alone with him. I walk out, unsure of what my next move in life is. If I just considered gutting a dog in order to save a wedding—a wedding for clients, not even friends of mine—I think it's clear I need to take some time out.

Chapter 6

Sunday 14th January

I can't believe I left that wedding yesterday. Thankfully, Jill stepped in to make sure the execution of everything went perfectly. Well, as perfectly as it can when your dog's eaten your rings. Apparently, Benny heaved and retched the whole way through the ceremony. It seemed to get a good laugh from the crowd with some saying he was revolted at all the love talk.

The bride and groom weren't best pleased with the rings their bridesmaid had managed to collect for them. The bride ended up with a diamanté Playboy Bunny ring and the groom had a Metallica Ninja Star ring. I mean, why were they inviting people like this to their wedding anyway? I think it's their own fault.

I'm woken from my glorious lie-in by my phone

ringing. Dammit, when will I learn to leave it on silent? I've only just spoken to Jill.

Hugh's name flashes up. Oh God. He's obviously heard about the farce that was yesterday and he's calling to give me a bollocking. I sigh. I could ignore it, let it go to voicemail, but then I'd only be delaying the inevitable. I take a deep breath and press accept.

'Hi, Hugh,' I say wearily into the phone.

I brace myself for this wrath. Don't get me wrong, he's not normally a shouty boss. I've got used to feeling like we're more partners than boss and employee. But that's part of the problem. I've become too comfortable with him.

Plus, I haven't had as much bad luck with weddings before as I have lately. He obviously thinks I'm taking my finger off the pulse.

'Hi Nads, how are you?' he asks, concern clear in his voice.

Nads? He never calls me Nads. I think back over the last year. Nope, I don't think I've heard him call me it once.

'Err... hi, Hugh.' I can't help but sound as thrown as I am.

'How are you feeling?' he asks, his voice soft and tender.

Am I imagining this phone call? Am I still asleep? Maybe dreaming the whole thing, including the nightmare dog scenario yesterday?

I decide to take the bull by the horns and address it

before he does.

'I take it you're calling about yesterday's wedding? You must have heard what happened?'

'Yeah,' I can almost feel his grimace. 'I popped in to lock up last night and Jill filled me in. Said you'd left.'

'I'm so sorry, Hugh. I don't know what got into me.'

'Don't worry about it, Nadine. I've put you under a lot of pressure over the last year and I often forget that you're a normal human being with limits. I mean, I can't remember the last weekend you had off. Can you?'

I wrack my brain. Well, we have weddings on weekends so it's not the right time.

'It's kind of a weekend job, though.'

'Regardless, Nadine. I think you expect too much from yourself. I want you to take a few days off.'

'You're... you're not firing me, are you?' I ask, my voice wobbling slightly.

He scoffs a laugh down the line. 'Of course not! Nadine, you'll always have a job here, for as long as it's open. I just think you need to de-stress a bit.'

'I'm really fine,' I insist. Jesus, he's acting like I *did* gut the dog. 'Has Jill said something to you?'

'No, why? What would she say?'

That I was close to gutting a dog.

'Oh, nothing.'

'I just want you to be nice and refreshed for cousin Clara's wedding. That's the one that really matters.'

I scoff. 'No pressure then, yeah, Hugh?'

He laughs down the phone. 'No pressure.'

But I know there is. I need to stop riding Hartley about his choices of marrying Clara, even if they do want different futures, because this wedding is turning out to be one of the most important of my career. So, I need to make sure it runs perfectly, regardless of any personal feelings.

I agree to having tomorrow off just to shut him up and end the call, jogging downstairs to make myself a cup of tea.

'You alright, love?' Mum asks, already in the process of making us both one. She's a good woman.

'Yeah,' I sigh, lifting myself up to sit on the counter. She raises her eyebrows at me. She's always telling me off for sitting like this, but she lets the cat walk all over the worktop and that's far more unhygienic. That thing licks her own arse. 'Hugh's just told me to have the day off tomorrow. Try to relax.'

She laughs. 'Even as a little girl, you've never been able to relax. You go from being "on" to sleeping. There's never been much in between.'

I sigh. 'I can't help how I am.'

'And you shouldn't apologise for it,' she says with a nod. 'After everything you've been through, you can't blame a girl for wanting to distract herself.'

'Gee, thanks, Mum,' I snort, taking the tea from her.

She sighs. 'You never want to talk about it but remember that it happened to all of us too.'

I sigh. I often forget that she lost her granddaughter too. But it's still different. She didn't feel that baby growing inside her for nine months. She didn't have her entire relationship break down and then have to move back to the family home. To say my life ended along with Belle's is an understatement.

'I'm sorry, Mum. I know you grieved too, but... I just don't want to talk about it.'

She smiles at me. 'Why don't we just relax today? You were so busy on the run up to Christmas we never had a chance to just sit around and watch Christmas films.'

'You're suggesting we watch Christmas films, in January?' I ask in amusement. 'Doesn't Lydia have a list of wedding jobs we need to get on with?' The woman's a slave driver.

She laughs. 'I've told your sister to start giving more of her jobs to her bridesmaids. They need to earn those expensive dresses.' I mean, she is right, but I can't believe she's told Princess Lydia that. Normally she can do nothing wrong. 'And why bloody not enjoy some Christmas films?' she laughs. 'It's still cold enough.'

I can't help but feel a massive affection towards her in that instant. I jump down and engulf her in my arms. Where the hell would I be without this woman?

'Let's do it.'

Monday 15th January

I'm back at the school today. It's so different being in a high school compared to the old primary school I used to work in. I actually feel self-conscious. I walk past a group of boys rehearsing, when they start wolf-whistling. Assuming it must be for one of the girls, I carry on walking with my head down.

'Alright, Miss?' one of them shouts towards me.

I turn to look at them and notice the main lad giving me a cheeky wink. I swivel to see if someone is behind me. Are they talking to *me?*

'You're a right fitty, Miss!' another one shouts. His mate barks out a laugh.

Well, what the hell am I supposed to do in this situation? You don't get this kind of crap with five-year-olds. I'm blushing before I can reason with myself to play it unaffected. And now I look like I'm enjoying it. They might even take it as encouragement. Think I'm a horny Mrs Robinson type who fancies a gang bang in the car park.

'Boys!' Hartley booms behind me. 'Leave Miss Roberts alone.'

I smile at him gratefully, hoping to God my cheeks aren't as heated as they feel. 'Thanks.'

'You can't blame them really,' he grins, like a teenage boy himself for a second. He quickly recovers himself and plasters on an impassive face.

'Huh?' Does he think I'm leading them on? Dressing slutty or something? I look down at my black pencil skirt and salmon blouse. It hardly screams harlot. In fact, I make a real effort to deliberately dress conservatively. I don't like exposing body parts, especially in the wedding industry. You don't want the grooms staring at your tits.

'I mean they're not used to seeing gorgeous teachers.'

Did he just call me gorgeous? What the hell is happening here?

'They're used to women in their fifties in lots of plaid.' He bends over in a chuckle.

Oh right. He wasn't calling me gorgeous. Just saying I'm better than a fifty-year-old. Hardly a raving review, the cheeky bastard.

I smile tightly. 'I *think* there's a compliment in there somewhere.'

He straightens up, attempting to wipe the smile off his face. 'There is.' He stares at me just a bit too long, our eyes connecting like magnets. He breaks away first, clearing his throat. 'I was thinking you could help with some painting of the props today. That cool with you?'

'Yep,' I nod, glad of the subject change. 'Fine by me.'

He shakes his head.

'What?' I can't resist asking. I want to know what he's thinking.

He scoffs a laugh. 'You're just so easy going. I'm not used to dealing with women without an argument in every conversation.'

I laugh. That's a little awkward. He's clearly talking about Clara. But I'm not falling into that trap again. Talking about her will only have him getting pissed off at me again. Better to ignore the bait.

And me, classed as laid back? That in itself is hilarious. If Florence was here she'd piss her pants laughing.

'Anyway, must get on.'

I rush over to where the paint pots are, some students already painting. Anna's there painting a tree.

'Hey,' she smiles, her big brown Bambi eyes troubled.

I casually walk up to her. 'Hi. How are you?'

She forces a cheery smile, looking around her to see if I'm drawing attention to her. 'I'm okay.'

I smile kindly, placing my hand on her shoulder. 'You don't have to lie to me, you know.'

She looks over at Hartley who's watching us intently. He quickly looks away. Discreet Hartley, *real* discreet.

'Does Sir know?' she asks, her eyes drooped, as if already knowing the answer.

'Yeah,' I nod with a grimace. 'I didn't tell him though,' I insist quickly. I don't want to lose her trust. 'He overheard us the other day.'

She sighs. 'I thought so. He's been treating me differently.'

Differently? I bloody hope not. If he's treating her like a little slut, I'll kick his arse myself.

'He's not being a dick to you, is he?' I ask, my voice rising despite me trying to talk myself down from the increasing anger growing inside me.

She snorts a laugh, then does an eye roll. 'No. He's just being a bit overprotective. Plus, I can see he's disappointed in me. Every time he looks at me it's as if I can see him thinking *"what wasted potential".*' She looks to the ground with a sad smile, her spine bowed over.

I rub her shoulder. 'He's not disappointed *in* you. He's disappointed *for* you, because he saw a bright future for you and he's scared it's all going to go down the toilet.'

She sighs. 'And is it? Am I doing the right thing?'

'What do you mean?' Do you want an...' I look around to make sure no one is listening. Luckily, they all seem oblivious. 'Abortion?' I whisper.

'No,' she says sternly with a shake of her head. 'But what if my parents don't support me? What if they force me to...' she looks around to check no-one is paying attention, 'you know. Get rid.'

God, the thought of parents forcing their daughter to do that makes me feel sick. Where the hell has the compassion in the world gone? But she must be overreacting. Everyone dreads telling their parents they fucked up, but the fear is normally worse than the aftermath.

'Surely they wouldn't?'

Her eyes fill up with tears. 'You don't know them,' she

says, her voice wobbling. 'They're strict Italian Catholics.'

Oh Jesus. I once went to summer camp with a girl from that background. She felt so bad after snogging Jake Weilders that she did the rosary. It took forever. So long I had to make new friends. Easy going sluts are far more fun, as it turns out.

'So surely they don't believe in... you know... the *other* option.'

She shakes her head about, clearly trying to pull herself together before anyone notices she's about to burst into tears. 'That doesn't mean they'd allow me to keep it after.'

After? Wait. She's not saying... no, she can't be.

I grab her arm and pull her over to the side, further away from everyone.

'Are you seriously telling me they'd make you go through a pregnancy only to then have it adopted?' I whisper-hiss, barely able to conceal my disgust.

She shrugs. 'I don't know. I could just be worrying for nothing. But, I just... I don't see them congratulating me.'

Okay, that sounds a bit more normal. She's clearly being a drama queen.

'They'd be weird if they did. But listen, if they try to force you into doing anything you don't want to do, then call me.'

'Why are you so nice?' she asks, crossing her arms across her chest, her body angling away from me. 'Are you trying to groom me or something weird you hear about on the news?'

'What?' I splutter. 'Of course not!'

Although I can't help but be impressed that she watches the news. So much potential.

'I was only joking,' she shrugs. 'Well, half-joking at least.'

'I guess I feel a little protective of you for some reason,' I admit, reminding myself not to get too attached. She isn't a temporary replacement for Belle.

'Do you have kids?'

The simple question that never fails to throw me. I steady myself, and try not to react, but it's hard when you feel as if you've been kicked in the heart.

'No, I don't.'

It's not a complete lie. I don't have any kids. That doesn't mean that I never did.

She smiles brightly at me. 'Well, you'll make an amazing mum one day.'

I feel the liquid pool in my eyes before I have a chance to reason with my emotions. I *was* an amazing mum. That didn't stop it from happening though.

'Thanks.' I shake my head, desperate to change the subject. 'So, are you going to tell me who the father is? Please don't tell me it's one of those tools.' I point over towards the lads that wolf-whistled me.

Her eyes fall to the floor. Oh crap. It is.

'No way!' I shriek, unable to hide my surprise. 'Which

one?'

'Ben Payne,' she admits on a sigh.

As if I know which one that is. I look over, just in case they're wearing name tags today. Damn it, just my luck.

'And I'm guessing you haven't told him?'

She shakes her head. 'Look at him. He's an idiot. There's no way he can help me. I can't believe I even did anything with him. But you know... vodka.'

I smile, patting her on the shoulder. 'I really do.'

At the end of the day I'm helping Hartley to clean up. It's shocking how much mess teenagers can make with just a bit of paint. I swear there's more paint on the floor than on the actual props.

'God, kids really are rubbish at tidying up after themselves, aren't they?' I moan, scrubbing off a particularly stubborn bit of dried on paint. I hope to God he was supplying them with washable paint and not the stuff you put on living room walls.

'Yeah, sorry. You shouldn't have to do this. I keep forgetting you're not actually on the staff. You go on home.'

'Oh, I don't mind.' More like I don't want to leave him. Or don't want to go home by myself to watch my parents cuddled up on the sofa. It's sad when you're jealous of your parents' relationship, with only the family cat for affection. And she's shit at conversation.

'So, I saw you talking to Anna earlier,' he starts, appearing to be vague. I know better. Here comes him digging for information from me.

'Yep,' I nod, choosing not to elaborate.

He waits for me to supply more information, but I avoid his gaze, forcing him to talk.

'Did she tell you who the father... no, scratch that, that makes it sound too mature for these idiots. Who the baby daddy is?'

I roll my eyes, but nod. 'Yes.'

He looks at me, waiting for more. 'And?'

'And I don't think I should tell you. She told me in confidence.'

'Oh, come on, they're kids!' he says sharply, his jaw tense.

It pisses me off that he can disregard her emotions so easily, just because she's only sixteen. If anything, at sixteen is when you feel the most emotions, all at once. Everything is the end of the world. Only in her case, it might just be.

'She may only be sixteen years old, but she has a wise head on her shoulders. She's going to be fine.'

He scoffs, eyes narrowed at me as if I'm mental. 'Jesus, do you live in cuckoo land? This is the worst thing that could have happened to her.'

I scoff back at him. Jesus, he's a drama queen.

'I really think you have the wrong perspective. She's pregnant, not dying.'

'Her future is!' he shouts, throwing his cloth back into the soapy water. 'God, why does it always happen to the ones with the most potential?'

I get that he's frustrated, but he needs to see that this isn't the end.

'If she works hard, she can have it all. Go to college or something. It'll just take longer than she originally thought.'

'Oh, don't give me that crap,' he barks back. 'You don't believe in all of that having it all stuff, do you? Be honest, one or the other always suffers.'

'Not always,' I snap, the feminist inside me flaring her nostrils in rage.

He rolls his eyes to the ceiling. 'We'll have to agree to disagree.'

I don't care what he says. I'm going to do everything in my power to ensure Anna has every opportunity possible open to her. If her parents or Hartley won't fight for her future, then I will.

'We'll just have to do that,' he snaps, taking the bucket and storming off.

Yeah, thanks for helping out tonight, Nadine. Arsehole.

Chapter 7

Tuesday 16th January

All of this thinking about Anna and her baby has me thinking about Belle a lot. Well, a lot more than normal. Of her little toes and her wrinkled fingers, her fingernails already so long. I remember holding her tight and studying every detail of her. But where there should have been warmth there was coldness. Where I should have felt her heart beating against mine, there was nothing but stillness.

When it happened, the idea of having another baby was so far away from what I wanted. I just wanted her back. Joshua wanted us to try again straightaway. As if I could just forget her and think oh well, I can always have another baby. Like I didn't just carry her for nine months: feel every kick, listen to every heartbeat at the scan, think of a possible name for her. He just didn't get it.

But now... I don't know. I'm scared to go through it all again, but my urge to have another baby is growing by the day. Even if the urge is only there for 'someday'. I'm all too aware that I'm thirty-two. Time is ticking away. In another few years my fertility will fall off a cliff according to those scaremongering health magazines I read.

So today I've decided to visit my doctor and find out where I stand with my biological clock. Get more of an idea.

'Miss Roberts,' the doctor calls.

I look up, braving a smile. The stern looking male doctor does a nod, barely recognisable to the human eye. I've met him before. That's his version of a beaming smile.

I stand up, gulp, and follow him into the small room. Being here brings back far too many memories. Memories of me crying, asking for something to help ease the pain.

The doctor sits down, crossing his legs in a very feminine way. 'So, Miss Roberts. What can I help you with today?'

I take a deep breath. 'I want to know the chances of me getting pregnant.'

His eyes widen ever so slightly, obviously surprised. 'Ah. I didn't realise you were in a new relationship.'

'Err... I'm not,' I admit bashfully. 'But, I'm very aware of my age and I just want to know the quality of my eggs.'

'Okay,' he nods, his face still not showing a hint of emotion. 'Well, unfortunately the NHS won't send you for a scan to assess the quality of your eggs until you've been actively trying with a partner for over a year.'

My shoulders sag. Bloody fantastic.

'But I can order a blood test to see if you're ovulating before your cycle?'

'Yes, please,' I nod. That's something I suppose.

'You can of course pay to go private and get the scan, but there are things you can do in the meantime to increase your chances. A healthy diet, cutting out alcohol, mild exercise.'

'Yeah, the usual,' I nod. All the things I did when I found out I was pregnant with Belle.

'There is also the risk of being on Fluoxetine while pregnant.'

I knew he was going to mention my Prozac. I've been on it since Belle and after about four long months I finally felt it bringing me back to my old self. Now I feel completely normal, able to hold down the burning emotions of my grief for long enough to get through the day.

Yet I'm terrified that if I come off it, I'll revert to how depressed and anxious I was. And the truth is that even if I only go back to five percent of how low I was feeling, it's not worth it. I can't go through that agony again.

'Would you recommend I come off it?' I ask, dreading his possible answer.

He raises his eyebrows in alarm. 'Of course, I wouldn't recommend that straightaway. You could have some serious side effects. Fluoxetine is one of the better studied antidepressants of pregnant women and it's unlikely to cause birth defects. But it is possible that if taken throughout the pregnancy a baby could develop neonatal adaption syndrome. That's when the...'

'No.' I shout cutting him off. 'I don't want to put any potential baby under any risk.'

He smiles sadly. 'Nadine, I understand with your history you'd be concerned, but you have to remember that you were suicidal at one point. It may be safer for you to continue with them during the pregnancy. It's far better for the mother to be mentally well.'

I scoff. 'Yeah, tell someone who's lost a baby that. Oh wait, you just did.' I can't help but be harsh.

'If you'd prefer, we could work on weaning you off it slowly, starting with reducing your amount?'

I twist my ring around my finger. That sounds a bit better. I want to do everything in my power to get my body in peak condition. Not that I have any idea who I'd have a baby with. Maybe I could get a sperm donor and do it on my own? I know my parents would help out.

'Weaning me off. How would that work?' I enquire.

He checks his computer. 'You currently take two 20mg tablets at night. I'd suggest alternate days where you only take one tablet.'

I at least expected him to suggest coming down by 10mg first, but a whole half a dose? That seems extreme.

'And will I have side effects?' I ask, already fearing

what I'm going to go through.

'You could possibly have some,' he nods, 'but Fluoxetine is the easiest SSRI to wean off due to the Prozac staying in your system longer. Give it a go.' He types on his computer, an awkward silence descending over us. 'But I notice that you never took up my offer of therapy. Without that you might not have the tools to cope.'

I snort. 'I don't need to sit in a room and tell some stranger how I'm feeling. I have my family and friends for that.'

He smiles tightly. It's his version of rolling his eyes. 'Okay. I can only suggest it. For now, would you like me to schedule in a blood test?'

A blood test? Oh, he means to check if I'm ovulating. I think about it for a moment.

'No thanks. I already know I can ovulate anyway, it's just to know how many quality eggs I have left. I'll probably go private. But I'll try to reduce my dosage in the meantime.'

He nods. 'Any problems, come back and see me.'

I walk out of there feeling both hope and worry. Hope that I can have another baby someday but worry over how my body will react to less drugs. Can I really cope with my own mind and grief without the drug I've come to rely on?

Wednesday 17th January

Last night was my first reduced dose. Only one tablet, instead of my regular two. I felt positive going to bed. He said I wouldn't get many side effects. I probably wouldn't notice a thing. This morning however, I woke up feeling awful. My head pounded with a heavy headache as I forced my tired limbs to get out of bed.

My hands shook, and I felt so agitated, so on edge.

I'd have stayed at home if I hadn't booked in cake testing with Clara and Hartley. Part of the service we offer at The Duck & Goose is to include everything so there's minimal stress for the bride.

So, I force myself to drive there, using every bit of deep down strength to pull myself together. Let me tell you, it takes a lot. I can't shake the feeling like something terrible is about to happen. The panic claws at my throat.

This can't just be from the reduced tablets, can it? Maybe it's women's intuition that something terrible is about to happen. God, I hope it's not Florence and the baby. I say a silent prayer to the God I don't believe in that she'll be okay. Not her.

I'm just finishing styling the cake portions, sure they don't look quite right, when suddenly my ear bristles from the cold outside.

'Boo.'

I nearly jump out of my skin, spinning round to see

Hartley looking at me with amusement dancing in his eyes.

'Jesus!'

Just the thing someone already living on their nerves needs, a shock.

He grins. 'Nope, I go by Hartley.'

Bloody idiot.

'God, you almost gave me a heart attack. How the hell did you sneak up on me without me hearing? You're a damn tree.'

He frowns, fighting the smile pulling on the edge of his lips. 'Sorry? Did you just call me... a tree?'

I burst out laughing, glad for any emotion over than fear. 'Let's be honest. You're a total tree.'

'As in...?' His raises his eyes, awaiting my answer, a hint of amusement in the side of his lips.

God, can he really not figure it out himself?

'You're all like... hench and stuff.' God, I don't want it to sound like I'm flirting with him.

'Oh yeah,' he grins playfully. 'Been checking me out, have ya?' He flexes his bicep in a jokey manner. 'I can't blame you.'

'Oh please,' I scoff with an eye roll, looking down at the cakes so I don't have to look him in the eye. 'I know some women are impressed by that, but not me.'

'Really?' he laughs.

I look back up at him, his forest-greens alight with humour.

'Yes, really.' Why is he even flirting with me when Clara should be walking in any second? 'Anyway, where is Clara?'

His turn to roll his eyes. 'She said she can't get the time off work. Sent me instead. More like doesn't want to eat any cake.'

'She doesn't eat cake?' I repeat in barely concealed horror. 'Not even wedding cake?'

He shakes his head. 'Nope. Even when we go out for dinner I end up eating desserts by myself.'

God, what kind of weirdo is she? Who the hell doesn't like cake? Is he sure she's not a robot? She clearly mustn't have feelings. Everyone with feelings has cried over a huge slab of cake while stuffing yourself silly.

'But I bet she steals half of it... right?' I mean, she must be a *woman.*

'No.' He shakes his head sadly. 'She's got ridiculous self-control.'

God, a woman who doesn't like cake. That idea is so foreign to me.

'Whereas I like dessert so much sometimes I order two and pretend one is for her.'

I snort a laugh. My kinda guy.

'I really wouldn't have put you two together,' I blurt out before thinking.

Oops, that didn't sound good. I can only blame the medication withdrawal. It's forcing me to be honest. I don't have the time or energy for too much bullshit right now. Not that I can tell him that.

He snorts. 'Gee, thanks.'

'Sorry, just... how did you even meet?' I ask, trying to move the conversation to something happier.

I'd imagine they run in completely different circles. Plus, the more I talk to him, the calmer my body is feeling, as if a serene mist is ascending over my body. It's probably having company and not just being stuck inside my own head, but regardless I don't want it to stop.

He smiles sadly, as if replaying the memory in his head.

'In a bar. She was on a hen do, dressed up ridiculously with a pink feather boa, and she asked if she could kiss me to win a dare.' He smiles, as if he remembers her being adorable. I have no idea how Clara could ever be seen as adorable. The woman doesn't eat cake for Christ's sake. 'She was a lot more chilled out then.' I bet. The thought of her wearing a jokey feather boa is enough to give me a stroke.

'So, what's changed?' I can't help but ask sarcastically, but come on, that isn't the woman I've met.

He shrugs and sighs heavily. 'I don't know. She's taken on more responsibility at her dad's company.'

I call bullshit. More responsibility doesn't mean you turn into a bitch. She's clearly always been one, and he's been too blinded by her vagina and tits to care.

'It's another reason why I definitely don't want to work there,' he elaborates, looking out of the window at the blustery day. 'It's not worth the stress.'

'And being a teacher is stress free?' I laugh hysterically. Jesus, I sound nuts. Maybe I am nuts? Maybe without the medication I'm a real regular fruit loop who shouldn't be allowed around sharp objects.

He joins me in a chuckle, thankfully not seeming to notice my hysteria. 'No, but it's different. You know that if you touch one student, it's all worth it.'

'You know you shouldn't touch students, right?' I joke. God, I'm *hilarious*. Maybe these meds have been holding me back from reaching my full potential as a stand-up comedian.

He shoves me playfully with his shoulder. I almost fall face first into the plate of cake, he's that strong.

'Hey! Remember your strength, Lenny!' I shout, creasing over in laughter.

'Lenny?' He frowns, his eyes narrowed at me in bewilderment.

I nod, shocked he's taking so long to get it. 'From of Mice and Men.'

'Oh... the book,' he finally nods.

'Jeez, you can tell you don't teach English.'

His eyebrows narrow as if suddenly realising something. 'Wait, wasn't he retarded?'

'No one says retarded anymore, idiot. You must have

missed the PC talk at work. He had... difficulties, yeah.'

He lowers his chin. 'And you're comparing me to him? Saying I'm all muscle and no brain?'

I snort a laugh. 'No, it was just a joke. But now you mention it...' I burst out laughing again. All of this laughing is calming my erratic heart.

'Do you always insult your clients like this?' he asks with raised eyebrows.

'Just the ones I like.' I wink. Jesus, why the hell did I just wink? Am I flirting with him? Openly flirting with him while he picks out his wedding cake? What the hell is wrong with me!

He stares at me as if trying to figure me out. I break away from his intense gaze, scared if he keeps looking he'll be able to see all my secrets.

'Anyway, cake. What flavours were you thinking?'

He shrugs, leaning on the bar. 'I don't know. Cake flavour.'

I roll my eyes. 'Jesus. This is going to be harder than I thought.'

'That's what she said!' he jokes.

I double over laughing. God, why are we both in such silly moods? Either way, it's distracting me from my panicky thoughts.

'Okay, let me be professional.'

He stands up straight and nods, a smile still on his lips.

'Let's start with a basic vanilla sponge with vanilla

icing and jam.'

I pick it up on its tissue, my hand shaking so badly I'm sure he'll notice, and hand it to him.

'Are you not going to feed it to me?' he asks, opening his mouth in a big 'O' shape. 'Or are you too hungover?'

'Hungover?' I snort. 'What are you talking about?'

He points to my hand. 'You're shaking. Big night out, was it?'

I can feel my cheeks reddening. Damn these withdrawal symptoms. A normal client, not as laid back as Hartley, wouldn't find it so funny.

'I didn't go out,' I insist.

'Okay, if you say so.' He rolls his eyes jokingly. 'So, feed it to me.' He pops his mouth open again.

'No. This cake isn't grapes and we aren't in ancient Rome.'

'Such a shame.' He takes the cake and wolfs it down in one go. The animal. Is it wrong that I find it sexual? Of course it is Nadine. The guy's getting married.

'Like?' I ask, my pen hovered over my review sheet on my clipboard.

'Yeah, it's nice,' he nods indifferently. 'But what else you got?'

I immediately strike that out. A man can't have a cake he finds 'nice' on his wedding day. It needs to be spectacular.

'Okay, we have a fruit cake next.' I hand it over to him.

He breaks it in half. 'Try it with me? I can't bear the way you look at me with anticipation while I chew. It's weird.'

I bark a laugh, but you don't have to ask me twice. I take the offered-out bit of fruit cake and eat it. Mmm, I love fruit cake. I just need a cup of tea with it.

'So?' I ask eagerly, some fruit still in my mouth.

He shrugs. 'Yeah, I mean, it tastes like fruit cake.'

I sigh. 'Don't you have a flavour in mind when you think of your wedding?'

He sighs. 'Nope. Do people actually think things like that?'

'Of course.' I insist. 'For some men it's the only thing they want input in.'

'That's bloody sad. You must deal with a lot of fatties.' I roll my eyes. 'Okay, what would your wedding cake be?'

He's challenging the wrong broad. This bitch has had her dream wedding uploaded to Pinterest since it was available online.

'Easy, lemon drizzle.'

'Lemon drizzle?' he repeats in barely concealed horror.

What the hell is wrong with lemon drizzle? I'll show him. I grab the sample and stuff it into his mouth, the icing squished around his lips.

'See, nice right?' I grin, barely able to stop myself from breaking out into belly laughs at the shock on his face.

He chews, because he has no choice. I really did shove

it in there. What's come over me? I need my Prozac, that's what.

'Wow, someone really likes lemon cake,' he says, still with a mouthful.

'Sorry,' I grimace. 'I'm... not really feeling myself today.' I fiddle with my clipboard, so I don't have to look him in the eye. 'So, look, do you like the cake? Or do you just want to blow off the whole wedding?'

He frowns, clearly taken aback. I really shouldn't have come into work today. This was a mistake.

'Why do you ask?' he says calmly. Too calmly. It fucks me off.

'I don't know.' Oh, fuck it. I might as well be honest. 'I guess you don't seem very happy. Most guys I meet that are about to get married look excited, not terrified whenever I mention it.'

He swallows down the last of the cake. 'Yeah, well, I bet most of those men chose to get married themselves.'

I swallow hard, confused. What does he mean, chose to get married themselves?

'Well you asked her, didn't you? That's as much choosing as I can think of.'

He smiles sadly at me. 'She proposed to me.'

'No way!' I can't help but giggle. That's Clara all over. Not relying on a man for anything.

He shoves my shoulder with his. 'It's not that funny!'

'Sorry, but just imagining her taking it into her own

hands gives me the giggles.' I snort another laugh. Especially because he's such a big strong man.

'Yeah, yeah, laugh it up.' He has the slightest hint of a blush on the top of his cheeks.

'Sorry. She is a force to be reckoned with. But you still didn't have to say yes.'

He raises his eyebrows. 'Didn't I? She asked me in front of everyone at her 30th birthday party. I doubt that would have gone down well.'

The girl's a psycho.

'Ah.' I suppose I can see how that would have made it that more awkward.

'It was all okay. I had it under control. We weren't planning on getting married for at least two years. I had time to figure out how to get out of it.'

'And then I called,' I say, filling in the blanks.

'Yep,' he nods. 'And all of a sudden I'm getting married in just over a month.'

'Fuck.'

'Yep, fuck indeed.'

But he can't blame it all on me. 'I'm sorry that me calling has put you in this situation, but...'

'But what?'

'Well you can't marry someone if you don't love them.'

'I do love her,' he says defensively. 'I just... I guess I love her like I would a best friend. I don't get those squirms in my stomach when I look at her anymore. It's like we've outgrown each other.' His eyes find mine.

God, he's beautiful. I can see why she'd be fooled into thinking he was in love with her if he's giving her looks like this.

'I think you really need to think it through. This is a big deal.'

'I know,' he says, his face pained. 'I just always imagined when I married someone I'd be totally, ridiculously, over the top in love with them. Not just... going with the flow.'

'You have to tell her.'

He closes his eyes tight. 'But I'll break her heart.' He opens them again, as if begging for me to understand. 'I'm not a heartless bastard. I don't want to humiliate her like this. Her family have already told half of England.'

I smile sadly back at him. It does sound tough, and I can understand what kind of pressure he's under. Hugh has already warned me that we can't fuck up this wedding and here I am telling him to walk away.

'I really shouldn't be encouraging you to do this anyway. I'm just here to plan your wedding.'

'And sort the costumes for my students,' he adds with a chuckle.

I laugh too. 'Yeah, I got talked into *that*. Good luck getting out of that engagement.'

He locks eyes with me, suddenly appearing serious. 'What if you were happy enough before and then something comes along to make you realise happy *enough* is not as happy as you want to be?'

Why is he looking at me so intensely? My pulse starts racing under the scrutiny of his gaze. Is he... no, he can't be talking about me, right?

He shakes his head, as if realising he just spilled his guts.

'Sorry for just sprouting all of that. It must just be pre-wedding nerves. You won't repeat it, will you?'

I force a smile. 'Of course not. Your secret's safe with me.'

Chapter 8

Thursday 18th January

I can't do it. I can't reduce my medication. Last night I was back to two tablets and the thought of only having one tablet tonight already has me twitching in anxiety. Why had I ever thought it would be easy? I was stupid to think I could attempt it before Lydia's wedding this weekend. Hopefully I'll be less of a basket case by then.

So maybe it turns out I'm not supposed to have another baby. Maybe Belle is my one and only. In a weird way that's kind of okay with me.

The thought of going through it all again just for the same fate to be repeated has my heart already detaching and attempting escape for fear of breaking again. I don't think I'd survive it a second time. At least now I can work on accepting a child-free future.

I'm barely in work when the phone starts calling, Clara's number flashing up at me. I knew giving her my mobile number was a mistake.

'Hi, Clara,' I say through gritted teeth.

'Hi,' she says brusquely. 'So, I've been thinking that I want ice sculptures.'

Jesus.

'Um, okay.' My voice comes out flat and uninterested. I shake my head, remembering to be professional. 'Sure, I know a contact. What kind of sculpture were you looking for?'

'I was thinking life-size sculptures of me and Hartley kissing. What do you think?'

That you're a crazy bitch who wouldn't know taste if it hit you in the face.

'Um... okay. I can get a quote for that.'

'Oh, money is no issue,' she says dismissively.

Of course, it isn't, not for Princess Clara.

'Okay. I'll call you back later then.'

Money is no issue. God, I'm used to dealing with brides on tight budgets. Not spoilt bitches like her. She *so* doesn't deserve Hartley. Whoa, where did that come from? I need to stop thinking about this soon to be married man.

I call up my supplier, Jenny, and tell her about Clara's idea.

'Classy,' she deadpans. 'So, we're looking at two grand, easy.'

'That's fine. She said money is no issue.' I eye roll as if she can see me.

'Well, isn't that nice for her,' she snorts. 'In that case, tell her three grand.'

I burst out laughing. 'Okay, I will.' The cocky cow deserves it.

She chuckles. 'If she agrees I owe you a night out!'

I'm barely off the phone when it starts buzzing again. I look. It's Clara. Of course, it is. There I was thinking my sister was the biggest Bridezilla I've come across.

'Hi, Clara. I just got off the phone with the ice sculptor.'

'Never mind that,' she snaps. 'Daddy wants to know if you can serve caviar?'

I grit my teeth to stop myself from growling. I hate being interrupted. My mum has always said, manners cost nothing. 'We can get that in for you, yes.'

'Fabulous. Also, I'm thinking about swans.'

I hold my now throbbing temples. 'Swans?' I repeat in disbelief.

'Yes. Wouldn't it be amazing to have a couple of swans wandering around? They're such majestic animals, don't you think?'

I wouldn't. I hate birds. Their beaks freak me out.

'Well, I'd have to check and see if we need any kind of licence to have them on site first.' Hopefully this will deter her.

'Nadine, darling, don't bore me with the details. Just let me know when you know, a simple yes or no.'

Rude bitch. *Don't tell her to go fuck herself. Don't tell her to go fuck herself.*

'Okay, fine,' I force through gritted teeth. 'I'll call you back.'

'Oh and is there any chance you could look into plastic surgery for one of my bridesmaids?'

'Sorry?' I must have misheard her. She wouldn't have just asked me about plastic surgery, right? Especially with less than a month until the wedding.

'My bridesmaid,' she explains, 'my dear friend, Jessica, has a huge nose, and she's been thinking about getting it fixed. I've offered to pay as long as it would heal before the wedding. We don't want that honker getting in the way of the photos!' She shrills a laugh.

I cannot believe this bitch.

'No. I'm afraid I don't look into cosmetic surgery,' I state firmly. 'That's gonna have to be you.'

'Okay. Speak soon. Ciao.'

Jesus, that woman is awful. Imagine offering to pay for your friend's surgery! What a heartless cow. I've barely opened my spreadsheet for suppliers when the phone's ringing again. This fucking woman!

'Hello?' I answer aggressively.

'Nadine, now I'm worried about the weather. Is there any way you can cover the entire outside area so if it rains no one will notice?'

Oh, for fuck's sake. Now this bitch wants me to do an anti-rain dance.

'Clara, you need to calm down.'

'Excuse me?' she asks, affronted.

Oops. I'm not used to telling my clients to calm down, but it just slipped out naturally. I can't help but be passive aggressive with her.

'What I mean is that regardless of the weather, you'll have a fantastic day,' I say brightly, attempting to salvage the situation.

'Well that's not what I asked is it?' she barks. 'I might just have to calm down and go somewhere else for my wedding.'

Oh crap. If I thought she was a pain before, pissed off Clara scares the shit out of me.

'That's not what I -' But it's too late. She's hung up on me. Great, just great.

The one client I'm not to upset, and I've just fucked her off royally. Fucking fantastic.

Friday 19th January

As I drag myself into the school, I have to remind myself why I'm even doing this. It's really not helping me stop thinking about Hartley and how he's mental to be marrying Clara. If anything, forcing myself to spend time with him is making me like him.

Don't get me wrong, I don't fancy the guy. Okay, that's a total lie. I fancy the pants off him. But that's all it is—he's good looking and fun to be around. But I'm not in love with the man or anything crazy like that.

It's not like I can back out of organising their wedding now. Especially after upsetting Clara. Hugh would kill me. If only their wedding would fall after he'd paid his uncle back, he wouldn't be so neurotic about it.

'Hi, Nadine,' Anna says as soon as I'm through the door, bounding over to me. 'I was hoping you'd be in today.'

'Oh, really?' I ask, intrigued. She's a lot more chipper than when I last saw her. Maybe she's told her parents and they've actually been really understanding.

'Yeah, I was wondering something.' She tucks a bit of blonde hair behind her ear, her eyes finding the floor before looking back at me with her eyebrows squished together, suddenly appearing shy. 'Would you... I mean, how would you feel about...'

After the day I've had I can't be beating around the bush with bullshit.

'Jesus, Anna. Just spit it out.'

Her face falls. Oh well now I feel awful. I forgot how sensitive teenage girls are.

'Well if you don't want to know!' she cries, turning to storm off.

I grab her arm softly to stop her. 'Sorry.' She turns back. 'I'm sorry, Anna. I'm just having a bit of a hard day.'

She sighs. 'That's okay. Trust me, I know how that feels.'

This poor girl is going through the biggest challenge of her life and here I am snapping at her just because I've had to deal with an arsey client.

'So, what did you want to ask me?' I smile, forcing myself to appear cheery.

She looks around to check no-one is within hearing distance. 'I wondered if you'd come with me for my scan,' she whispers.

My mouth drops open. Her baby scan? Surely, she's not that far along yet, is she?

'Are you twelve weeks already?' I ask, my voice barely audible, my mouth is so dry.

'I will be next week,' she confirms, tucking more hair behind her ears. 'According to the midwife woman, who totally judged me by the way.'

'No way?'

'Yep,' she nods. 'She kept asking me if I was sure I wasn't interested in a termination.'

My hackles rise, my nostrils flaring in a fresh wave of rage. 'She *what?* How bloody dare she!'

She nods, her big brown doe eyes staring up at me. 'And then when I said I was keeping it, she just assumed I'd be giving it up for adoption. Started giving me leaflets about it.'

'Are you serious?' I almost shout, anger coursing through my veins. 'Who the hell is this midwife? Talk about a bitch. You should put in an official complaint.'

She shrugs in despair. 'I wouldn't know where to start.'

I'm already googling it on my phone.

'But anyway, would you come with me?' Her Bambi eyes look up at me hopefully.

'Of course. I don't want anyone else being a dick to you.' I can't believe how protective I feel for this girl in such a short time of knowing her.

She snorts. 'Thank you. I just... I don't think I can trust one of my mates to keep it a secret, and it's not like I can ask my parents.'

So, she hasn't told them then.

I bite my lip. 'You are going to have to think about telling them though, you know? You'll start showing soon.'

She shakes her head. 'I can't think about that right now. I want to get this scan out of the way. Make sure everything's alright before I think about what I'm going to do.'

Jesus, another anxious pregnant woman to deal with. Only this one isn't even a woman yet, she's still a girl.

She gives me her number and promises to text me the full appointment details.

I find Hartley practically pulling his hair out during the rehearsal. His glossy blonde locks are spilling from his top

knot from the amount of times he's run his hands over it in despair.

'No!' he shouts. 'How many times, Harry? The line is Peace, peace, Mercutio, peace! Thou talk'st of nothing.'

Harry shrugs. 'Is it really such a big deal?'

Hartley bristles. 'Oh, of course not,' he grunts sarcastically. 'In fact, why bother with the lines at all? Why not just make it up as we go! It's only Shakespeare, the most influential writer of all time. In fact, why bother with outfits when we can wear pyjamas?'

Jesus, the man has lost it. For the first time I can see why he teaches drama. He's a total queen.

'Alright there, Mr Valentine?' I ask behind him, trying hard to hide the smirk on my face.

He turns, shocked at the interruption. 'Great.' he snaps, jerking his head back dramatically. 'Bloody fantastic.'

I raise my eyebrows, unable to hide the snicker on my lips. 'I really think you should calm down.'

'Yeah,' he snorts. 'Because we all know the way to calm someone down is to tell them to bloody calm down. You might as well piss on a burning building, for all the good it'll do.'

I look back at the kids. They seem exhausted, leaning on the props just to get some sort of rest. Shakespeare's hard to understand at the best of times.

'I'm taking Sir for a coffee break. You guys relax for a

minute.' I start leading him away, pushing against his shoulder. It's hard when he's such a tree.

'Or read your lines!' he shouts back. 'Something that could actually help.'

I roll my eyes at the kids, causing a few to laugh.

'Jesus, Hartley, you need to calm down. You're going to give yourself a heart attack.'

He clenches his jaw. 'Don't you go starting on me. I've already had Clara on the phone screaming that you told her to calm down.'

I grimace. 'Yeah... that was a mistake.'

'Well someone here has to bloody care about this play, otherwise the whole thing will go to shit. And it's my name against it.'

Jesus, it's a school production, not a show in the West End.

We make it to the deserted staff room where I fill up the kettle and press boil.

'But really... it is just a school play. It's not like this is the West End. Parents are only going to expect so much.'

He shakes his head. 'You have no idea. We have talent scouts coming. This could be the difference between some of my talented students getting a scholarship to a drama school, or them ending up doing drama at a mediocre college.'

I smile back at him, shocked and impressed at his passion.

'You really do care about these kids, don't you,' I state more than ask.

He rakes his hand through his hair. 'Of course, I do. I wouldn't be in this job unless I did.'

I smile. 'Yeah, the pay and the hours aren't the most appealing otherwise,' I admit with a chuckle.

'Do you ever miss it?' he asks seriously, his eyes holding me in place.

I think back to those adorable little faces I left behind. After losing Belle my heart was no longer in it. Looking at those beautiful happy little faces used to uplift me, but it quickly turned to sadness. My Belle would never make it to reception class. She'd never go on to secondary school. Have a prom. Get married. Have a child of her own.

God, just thinking about it again has the hurt twisting inside me, making my eyes tear up.

'Sorry,' he says, his eyes darting from side to side in panic. 'I didn't realise something happened to make you leave.'

I force a laugh. It comes out sounding bitter. 'Nothing happened. At my work, anyway.'

He frowns. 'Oh. So... why are you upset?'

I think about telling him, but I can't. I don't know him well enough and I like the idea of him knowing a version of me that isn't drowning in her own grief.

'Something happened in my personal life that made me look at work differently. Made me look at everything differently really.'

He looks me in the eye, holding eye contact for longer than is necessary. It feels impossible to look away, as if our eyes are magnets drawn together by a force stronger than us.

'I can see the pain in your eyes.'

I blink, as if I can dislodge the connection between us. I shake my head. 'I'm fine.'

He smiles, his forehead wrinkling. 'I never said you weren't. Doesn't mean you haven't been through shit in your life.'

God, he really needs to stop saying such honourable things in front of me. It's not helping my crush. But God, when he talks to me it's as if nothing else in the world exists.

'Yeah, well, that's part of the reason my heads all over the place at the minute,' I admit. 'I've been trying to reduce my anti-depressant dose and... well, it's not going well.'

God, why am I telling him this? What is it about him that makes me want to spill my secrets?

'Shit,' he says, clasping my hand with his giant one. God, it's warm. I feel it all the way down my spine.

'I mean, don't worry or anything!' I quickly say, throwing my hands up to break the contact. No good will come from him touching me. 'I'm not some nutter that's going to freak out and kill everyone.'

His eyes soften with concern. 'I'd bloody hope so too,' he chuckles.

The door suddenly bursts open, Harry out of breath.

'Sir, Karl is fighting with Ben!'

'Oh, for fuck's sake.' He rolls his eyes at me. 'Back to work.'

Chapter 9

Saturday 20th January

Today is Lydia's wedding. I still have no idea how this day crept up on me so fast. Or how my baby sister is getting married before me. She didn't want to get married at The Duck and Goose so is instead getting married at a local manor house.

As I look up at the columned building, the gravel crunching under my feet, I wonder again how our parents afforded this. My mum's a dental nurse and my dad's an accountant. Hardly millionaires. I dread to think if they've put this on a credit card. But nothing's too much for Princess Lydia.

I carry her dress bag into the reception, following Lydia up the sweeping staircase and into the enormous bridal suite. I place the dress hanger on the curtain rail, hoping it's not creased. I brought my portable steamer just in case.

Lydia's already getting set up, with her friend doing her make-up. Mum's fussing around her, taking room service orders. I busy myself with steaming her dress (it needed it), topping up the glasses of Prosecco and placing the room service order.

We've just settled down with our food when Lydia bites into her flatbread, shrieks and covers her mouth.

'My tooth!' she shouts. 'Ah, motherfucker!'

'Language, Lydia!' Mum shouts, like she's still fifteen.

'Jesus, Lyds. What's happened?' I shriek. I know the girl is dramatic, but this is ridiculous.

'That bread is rock solid. Has it chipped my veneer?' She opens her mouth to show me her front tooth, chipped just like the day she first got it from the piggy back I gave her on her twenty first birthday.

'Fuck.' She looks like a homeless person.

Her eyes widen. 'What? What?' She starts running around searching for a mirror.

Mum looks at me, her eyes almost popping out of their sockets. I know she wants to say, *'What the hell are we going to do now?'*, but she's attempting to remain calm.

A piercing scream comes from the bathroom. I wince.

'Well, she's seen it,' I say to mum, with raised eyebrows.

She comes running out. 'I look like a fucking monster.

What the hell are we going to do?' She's looking at me like I have all the answers.

I walk to her, attempting to play it calm. 'It's fine. I'm going to get you an emergency dentist and they're going to fix it all.'

Her nostrils flare. 'Nadine, I get married in three fucking hours! I'm never going to get this sorted by then!'

'Not with that attitude,' I snap, tempted to slap her in order to calm her down. 'We literally don't have time for your tantrum right now.'

I get my phone out and update my Facebook status.

Emergency dentist needed! If you know one, please let me know ASAP

I quickly Google emergency dentists nearby and start calling them. I'm getting nowhere. They keep saying they're fully booked and referring me to each other.

I check back on Facebook and see that someone has recommended an uncle of theirs. I call the number, tapping my foot impatiently.

'Hello, Paragon dental,' a cheery lady answers.

'Hi, I have an emergency. I'm a friend of Sarah Lomas. My sister is getting married in two-and-a-half hours and she's just chipped her veneer. She needs a new one put on before the wedding. Sarah recommended you. Is there any chance you can fit her in?'

'Oh dear,' she says, tapping loudly on her computer. 'Okay, if you bring her straight in we can move some things around and see her straightaway.'

'Oh my God, I could kiss you! Thank you so much!'

I hang up and turn to a hopeful looking Lydia. 'We're going to the dentist now.'

She throws on some jogging bottoms and a jumper and grabs her bag. 'Let's go.'

We race towards the Harrow based dentist, parking hastily outside.

A man with hairy nostrils welcomes us and looks into her mouth. She's squirming every time he touches her and a fine sheen of sweat sits on her forehead. I forgot she's scared of the dentist. The baby.

'Right, we'll only be able to give you a temporary crown today. I'd suggest you contact your regular dentist after the wedding to get a cast made for your new permanent tooth.'

'Yeah, whatever. I just want it done now.' She says stroppily. 'I can't get married looking like a crack addict.'

'Please,' I add, with a sweet smile. It must help that my teeth are perfectly brushed and flossed.

'Wait,' Lydia says standing up. 'I remember it last time. The filing down hurt. I need some gas and air.'

'Okay,' he nods. 'If you feel it would relax you, I can give you some.'

'Yes please,' she says nodding frantically.

She gladly lies down now, taking the small nose mask and helping it be attached. She sniffs in slowly.

'Agh, I'm already feeling calmer.'

'Good.'

He starts trying to file the tooth, but she screams. 'Wait, I need more!' She inhales a few strong deep breaths.

The dentist turns to me. 'Maybe it would be best if you waited outside.'

'Sure.' You didn't have to tell me twice. I didn't want to witness this shit show.

I go to the waiting room and take call after call from concerned family and friends asking if she'll make it. I bloody hope so. We only have two hours left.

An hour later the dentist finally appears. About bloody time.

'There's been a bit of an unforeseen problem,' he admits with a grimace, his eyes unable to meet mine.

'Ri...ght?'

Oh Jesus, has she got no tooth at all now? The trauma from it damaged the nerve and now she's toothless? We'd *have* to cancel the wedding.

'I managed to fit the temporary crown.'

'Oh, thank the Lord,' I say sighing in relief. 'So, what's the problem? Do you not take credit cards?' I dread to think how much it has cost.

'No, we do.' He wrings his hands together. 'It's your sister. She seems to have had... quite a reaction to the gas and air.'

I frown back at him. 'What do you mean?'

'I mean,' he grimaces rocking from foot to foot, 'I can't

get her off the chair.'

I stare back at him, dumbfounded. I follow him back into the room. Lydia's sprawled on the chair, smiling back at me, looking happy as Larry.

'Nadwine,' she slurs. 'My twooth is all better.'

Oh Jesus. She's bloody shit-faced on the stuff.

'Yes, all better,' I agree, speaking to her as I would a child. 'Let me just pay the dentist and we'll get you back to the manor house.'

'You're the bwest.' She smiles, exposing her new perfect looking tooth. Well at least that's something.

I drag the dentist out. 'How much did you bloody give her?'

He puts his hands up in surrender. 'I'm sorry, but people don't normally react this strongly to it.'

'The woman's getting married in an hour,' I hiss. 'When will she go back to normal?'

He shakes his head, scratching the back of his neck. 'It's impossible to tell. It differs from person to person.'

'Jesus, what kind of back street dentist are you?' I shriek in horror.

'I'll have you know that I'm fully qualified!' he says, quickly, in a furious tone.

'Well I'm not paying you until she's been able to go through with her wedding. Let me assure you that it cost a hell of a lot more than this appointment and took my parents a year to save for.'

'Fine,' he says through gritted dentist perfect teeth.

He somehow manages to help get her up out of the chair and into my car, amused builders across the road laughing the whole time. Yeah, thanks for your help fellas. Who says chivalry's dead, hey.

I drive back while she snoozes in the car occasionally shouting out random words like "condom" or "mango". I'm hoping the sleep will help it wear off quicker.

When we finally arrive at the manor house we've only got thirty minutes until the wedding ceremony starts. I have to call Carolyn, her bridesmaid, to help me get her out of the car as she's not waking up. I'd be more worried she was unconscious if she wasn't snoring so loudly.

We loop her arms around our shoulders and walk her into the grand lobby. Some guests are milling around.

'Lydia. Congratulations.' One lady shouts.

Jesus, can she not see that Lydia's feet are being dragged along the floor?

'Lydia's a little unwell right now,' I say with a tight smile. 'Hurry along inside and she'll be down soon.'

She gives me a strange look but disappears, thank goodness.

We drag her up the sweeping staircase, the whole time me swearing how ridiculous it is for a big venue like this not to have had a lift installed. Grade II listed buildings are impossible. Move with the times people!

Mum opens the suite door, her eyes bulging out of

their sockets when she spots Lydia.

'What the hell did you do to her?' she accuses.

'Nothing.' I snap. Jesus, at least I've been trying to save the situation. 'It's gas and air from the dentist.'

'Oh, for goodness' sake. She can't handle gas and air. I remember she had it when she was twelve and she was giddy and talking rubbish for days.'

'Days?' I squeal. 'He said it should start to wear off.'

'Pineapples are strange,' Lydia says with a giggle.

Mum rolls her eyes. 'Well, she's getting married in half an hour. I don't expect for this to fix itself in that time. Honestly, Nadine. I would have thought you'd have remembered that.'

'This isn't my fault,' I protest, my lip curling up in rage. 'If you want to blame something then blame the flatbread.'

She sighs. 'Well, us bickering isn't helping anyone. Let's get her a coffee and then into her wedding dress.'

'Oh, is someone getting married?' Lydia asks. 'I'm getting married too!'

Jesus, fuck.

Forty minutes later and she's somehow in her wedding dress, ready to walk down the aisle. She's still high as a kite, but we have no other alternative. Dad's been warned to help her stand up. It's either this or cancel the wedding and that just isn't an option.

I take a deep breath and walk down the aisle ahead of her in my sky-blue bridesmaid dress, smiling politely at all of the friends and family. I know what they're thinking; I see the sympathy in their eyes. *Poor Nadine. It must be hard for her to see her younger sister get married. And after everything she's been through.*

When I reach Jason, I pretend to kiss his cheek, but instead whisper in his ear 'She's fine, just go with it.'

He stares back at me with raised eyebrows. I don't have a chance to say anything further, just stand to the side and watch Lydia and my dad walk down the aisle to the traditional wedding march.

She's smiling, all dopey happy, stumbling every few steps. Luckily, dad has a firm grip of her, so she doesn't go down. I wonder if she looks normal to everyone else that's none the wiser. Or maybe just a bit pissed from champagne.

She finally stands in front of Jason, handed over by my dad.

She giggles. 'Hey, sexy,' she whispers to Jason. I take her bouquet from her, warning her with my eyes.

The registrar starts talking as Lydia sways on her feet. Jason is watching her in confusion. He leans in and whispers 'Are you drunk?'

'Of course not,' she giggles. 'Just been eating pineapples.' She snorts. 'Did you know when I was younger I thought pineapples were pine cones with apples? How dumb was I?'

'Sssh.' I hiss at her, looking round to see if anyone has noticed.

'If anyone objects, let them speak now or forever hold their peace,' the officiant declares with a confident smile.

Please, don't let her say anything stupid.

I keep quiet, praying to God no one makes a sound. Always a tense time at a wedding.

'I object!' Lydia shouts with a giggle. 'I'm too young and sexy to be getting married.'

Oh, dear Lord.

A few awkward laughs echo around the room.

'Only joking,' she says with a snort laugh. She sounds like bloody Peppa Pig.

'Right,' the officiant says, clearly at a loss. 'I'll continue then.'

Lydia gets through the wedding, and by the time the speeches happen she's slowly getting back in touch with reality. Hopefully by the end she'll be completely her normal self. I do my brief speech and raise my glass of champagne to toast the happy couple, glad we pulled it off.

'Woo!' Lydia says, with her glass in the air as everyone cheers. 'And he's hung like a fucking donkey.'

Dear Lord.

Sunday 21st January

Today I've decided to meet up with my friend Amy. I met her through SANDS, a charity to help women that have had stillborn babies. We'd both lost babies around the same time and we formed such a strong bond that it would be weird to ever lose touch.

Just knowing there's someone that's been through the same thing as me, is such a relief. Don't get me wrong, Flo and the girls, were fantastic, but they don't know the pain. Until you do it's impossible to appreciate.

I knew in advance, with it being Lydia's wedding yesterday, that I'd be feeling low. I was right. Don't get me wrong, I'm so happy for her. But there is a part of me—deep, *deep* down—that is kind of giddy happy that she was high on gas and air and therefore didn't get her perfect wedding. See, I'm a bitch. This is why bad stuff happens to me.

Amy chats to me, not just about depressing stuff, but about new things in our lives. She seems to have such a great support system from her husband, Gary. That's something I'm severely lacking. In a strange way I actually feel more depressed now than I did at the beginning.

I hug her goodbye and leave the warm cafe to walk into the bitter-cold high street, wrapping my coat extra tight around my waist. Sometimes I really wish I had a man. Not to have them piss all over the toilet seat or pick up their smelly socks, but the rare moments where you can just lay together and be comforted by their mere presence.

'Nadine?'

I look up to find Hartley walking towards me in a stunningly sophisticated dark grey wool coat.

'I thought it was you,' he says on a smile.

'Oh, hey. You alright?' I even sound sad, deflated. My bones suddenly ache from exhaustion, the thought of putting on a fake happy face too much for me right now.

'Yeah, just getting a few groceries,' he says cheerfully. 'What about you?'

'Just catching up with a friend.'

I'm ready to turn and leave, but it's at that exact moment I see my ex, Joshua, over his shoulder walking towards us. Oh my God. This is a fucking disaster.

'Quick! Hide me!' I panic, looking from left to right. I could run back into the cafe, but that's window fronted so there's still the chance he'd notice me. I can't walk into traffic. 'Agh!'

'Err...'

He must think I'm mental.

In a last-ditch attempt at hiding I grab the sides of his coat and try to hide underneath them, pushing my face against his chest.

Please don't see me. Please don't see me.

'Nadine?'

Well fuck-a-doodle-doo. He's seen me after all.

I wince my eyes shut, horrified that I'm going to have to face this humiliation head on. I pull my head back out of Hartley's poor chest to see his bewildered face. He must think I'm unstable. Correction, madder than he originally thought I was.

I turn to where the voice came from. Joshua looks back at me, a friendly smile making his face look as beautiful as the day I first met him. How is that fair? Why couldn't he have aged terribly? Instead his fair hair seems thicker, his eyes kinder.

'Hi,' I say, my voice barely audible.

'Wow, it's been what? Three years?'

'Has it?' I screech, my voice now so high I'm sure only dogs can hear it.

He nods. 'Must have been. I heard you're planning weddings now. That must be hard. You know, seeing all of those happy couples.'

Did he really just say that? Talk about adding salt to the wound, pouring in petrol and then setting it on fire. He dumped me. At the one time in my life when I needed him.

'I enjoy it, actually.' I wanted it to come out as strong, defiant, but instead I sound like a church mouse. Damn it.

'Who's your friend?' he asks, nodding towards Hartley whose jacket I still have in my hands.

I look up at him, completely dumbfounded by the situation. I open my mouth to speak, but it's like nothing will come out. Instead I just stare at him, eyes widened in panic.

Hartley leans forward and shakes Joshua's hand confidently. 'Hartley Valentine. Good to meet you.'

Joshua looks between us, obviously intrigued as to why I'm spending my time with such a gorgeous man. Don't get me wrong, Joshua is gorgeous, but nothing compared to Hartley.

'And...' Joshua says, rocking on his heels. 'Do you two know each other well?'

I swallow hard, my throat suddenly dry.

'I should hope so,' Hartley chuckles, wrapping his arm around my waist. What now? What is he doing? 'She's marrying me.'

My mouth drops open of its own accord. He must mean that I'm marrying him and Clara. But then why does he have his arm draped intimately around my waist? Could it be he's pretending to save me from my obvious embarrassment?

'Wow,' Joshua says, completely taken aback.

Alright, there's no need to be that shocked. He might be gorgeous, but I resent the fact that he thinks I couldn't pull someone this fit if I wanted to. I'm not bloody ugly. I'm just not looking for someone. Anyone. Well, I wasn't until the gorgeous Hartley came along and reminded me how to feel.

'Wow,' Joshua says again. 'Congratulations.'

'Thanks,' Hartley gushes, pulling me closer. 'We're over the moon.' He looks back down at me adoringly. I just about manage to stare back at him with my mouth shut.

Joshua looks behind us. 'Ah, here comes my wife.'

It's no surprise to me. I heard they got married within a year of him leaving me. Yes, it was devastating to hear about him moving on so easily, but I've gotten over it. He deserves to be happy too.

I turn my head to see a gorgeous brunette walking towards us. Well, waddling. She looks about eight months pregnant. Oh my God.

'Ariana, this is Nadine,' he says. 'And her fiancé, Hartley.'

Ariana's eyes widen. 'Oh wow. That's great news. And obviously you can see ours,' she laughs, pointing to her bump.

He's having another baby. I know it shouldn't, but it hurts. It hurts like a bitch. If Belle hadn't died would we still be together? Would we be married? Planning a second baby? Tears prick at my eyes, but I shake my head, praying to God my tear ducts will pull themselves together.

'Anyway,' Hartley says, 'we must get going. Nice to see you.'

He takes my hand and drags me away. I move as if on autopilot, my legs moving but my mind elsewhere. We walk down the street in silence for a while until he pulls me into a small alleyway between shops.

He leans me against the wall and takes my face in his freezing cold hands. 'I hope you didn't mind me doing that.'

I shake my head, still unable to form words.

'It's just that I could tell he was your ex, and a total

douche nugget.'

I laugh, despite my depression. 'Douche nugget? I can honestly say that's the first time I've heard that.'

He grins. 'Remember I'm around teenagers all day. You pick up the slang.'

I smile, glad he's been able to pull me out of my funk through his choice of ridiculous insults.

'Tell me, did Fetch ever happen?' I ask, thinking about my favourite teenage movie, Mean Girls. I'm sure he won't get the reference.

He frowns, suddenly serious. 'No, Nadine. Fetch is never going to happen,' he grins.

Wow, he gets my Mean Girls reference. He's a keeper. For Clara, obviously. She's like the Regina George of this story.

'I saw you freak out when you saw her pregnant. I'm assuming that was a shock?'

I nod. 'Yeah, I just... I hadn't heard is all.' I shake my head, needing to get out of here. I can't have him interrogating me and finding out anything about my past. 'Anyway, I really need to go.'

I turn to leave, but he pulls softly on my arm. I look back to him, his face solemn.

'Nadine, I know we're not even really friends, but I'm here, you know. If you ever want to talk.'

Great, the guy thinks I'm suicidal.

I nod, and then scurry off as quickly as I can.

Chapter 10

I'm still feeling low today and mortified whenever I think of Hartley seeing me like that, at my lowest, but I have to keep wearing a fake smile as I have Clara's make up trial with Florence. I feel strangely like a slut whenever I look at Clara, knowing just yesterday her fiancé was pretending to be mine.

'Now,' Clara, says halting Flo, 'I want to know what products you plan on using. I have highly sensitive skin. I can only use MAC.'

Of course, Princess Clara has sensitive skin. I'm sure she only uses products made with unicorn tears and elf droppings.

Flo grimaces a smile. 'Luckily for you, I have a wide range of MAC products. Now, what were you thinking about for your wedding look?'

She grabs the mirror, any excuse to look at herself. 'I want full on glamour. I'm thinking dark smoky eyes and a blood red lip.'

'Okay,' Flo nods, giving me the quickest of glances. Only I can tell from it that she means to call Clara a high-maintenance whore.

She does her make-up, the whole time with Clara complaining that Florence wasn't putting on enough make-up/too much make-up/spending too much time/not enough time.

'Good luck planning her wedding,' Flo snorts as soon as she's left. 'That's one high-maintenance bitch.'

I blow out a held-in breath. 'Tell me about it.'

'And to think we're cousins-in-law. If that's how she treats me, imagine a normal make-up artist!'

I snort out a laugh.

'What's Hartley like?' she asks, starting to pack away her kit. 'He must be a saint to put up with her.'

'He bloody well is! I know you didn't get a chance to chat at the food tasting, what with you vomiting everywhere.' I stop to smirk quickly. 'But surely you've chatted before at some family function of Hugh's?'

'No.' She shakes her head. 'We don't have much to do with them to be honest. I'm sure you can see why.'

'Hartley's a bit of an idiot really. I don't think he even wants to marry her. Did you know that she proposed to him?'

Her eyes nearly bulge out of her sockets. 'She did not! That's so embarrassing.'

'Alright,' I snap, feeling slightly bad for her. 'Not all men propose to us on our first date,' I joke, reminding her how lucky she was to have found Hugh. Their engagement story still makes me laugh. They got engaged on their first date.

'Still,' she muses, 'I'd rather die than propose myself.'

I think about the position Clara's put him in. That's why the guys are supposed to propose. They're the ones that are so scared of commitment.

'Yeah. I do feel sorry for him.'

Flo's eyes become inquisitive. 'Why are you blushing?'

'Huh?' I'm not, am I? I touch my cheeks, they do feel a bit hot.

'You're *so* blushing. Do you... fancy him or something?' she asks, a grin playing on her lips.

Oh no, she's onto me.

'Don't be ridiculous.' I snort. 'He's getting married.'

She scoffs. 'Yeah, to someone you just said he doesn't really want to marry.'

'Well, that doesn't matter,' I insist, crossing my arms over my chest. 'I'm their wedding planner. It's my job to get them down the aisle without a hitch. End of story.'

'Okay,' she shrugs with a knowing smile. 'If you say so.'

'Don't have Hugh hear you saying that. He says we've got to take special care of this couple.'

'Really?' she frowns. 'Why?'

Uh-oh. I'm assuming she doesn't know about Clara's father lending Hugh money. I don't want to get him in trouble and have her worrying. Especially in her condition.

'Oh, just because... she's his cousin.'

She snorts. 'Whatever. I'm just glad they're not close enough that we have to eat Sunday dinner with them. I've got to know her more today than I have all year.'

'I'm sure she's nice deep down.'

She giggles. 'Deep, *deep* down. Anyway, I have some exciting news.'

'Really?'

She beams at me, suddenly full of excitement. She goes into her purse and hands over a piece of paper to me. I look down to see a baby scan. No way!

'You had a scan?' I blurt out.

'Yep!' she squeals. 'Only ten weeks, but they've assured me that everything is looking good.'

I throw my arms around her and squeeze tight. 'I can't believe you and Hugh are having a baby. It's so weird when you see it in the scan.'

Her eyes mist over, completely overwhelmed. 'I can't believe it either. It feels so real now. Are you sure you're okay about it?'

I frown, bewildered. I still feel so bad that she even has

to consider whether I'd be happy for her.

'Of course, I'm okay about it.' I rub her arm with affection. 'You're my best friend and you're having a baby. I'm so happy for you guys and no past grief will ever affect that.'

'You sure?' she checks, pulling me into a weird kind of side hug.

'Of course. Do I miss Belle?' Jeez, just saying her name causes physical pain to my heart. 'Of course, but she's sent down a little angel for my bestie. I can't wait to meet them.'

Her eyes mist over. 'I love you. We were hoping you'll be godmother, if all goes well, of course.'

That nearly makes me cry, my throat clogging up. 'Of course, I will. And don't be thinking like that, everything will be perfect. I promise.'

Heartbreak can't strike twice, right?

Tuesday 23rd January

I hold Anna's hand as she lies on the bed, the nurse squirting the jelly onto her stomach. It feels so weird to think my bestie was here only a few days ago. I look down at Anna's stomach. She has no bump whatsoever so far. I bet she's not even taking prenatal vitamins.

'I really need a pee,' she whines, her face scrunched up

in an attempt to hold it in.

'I know,' I nod with a smile. 'It's all that water you've drunk.'

'Right,' the nurse says, putting the wand onto her stomach, making Anna flinch. 'Let's have a look at baby.'

I really didn't think it would be so difficult coming today, but the whole thing is just reminding me about Belle and the excitement I felt while carrying her in my stomach. It's funny, but I wasn't nervous at my first scan. And just as predicted everything went well. Nobody was to know what would happen.

'Is everything okay?' Anna asks, already the anxious mother.

'It's all looking fine,' the nurse nods back cheerily. 'From this I'd make your due date 7th August.'

At least it will be in the summer holidays, I can't help thinking to myself.

Anna looks back at me with a nervous smile. 'OMG, it all feels so real now.'

'That's because it is,' I smile, taking her hand and giving it a reassuring squeeze. 'You're going to be a mummy.'

Her face pales and she leans her head back on the bed, as if the realisation has hit her all at once. 'Yeah.'

The nurse cleans her up quietly, having sensed the change in mood, and prints out some pictures for her.

We're walking towards the car when I ask her. 'What's

wrong?'

'You mean, apart from being pregnant at sixteen?' she asks, her eyes downcast.

I smile. 'Yes, apart from the obvious.'

'I just...' she looks down at her stomach, her hand cradling it. 'Seeing it, it's made it all so real. I've got only six months to get my life together before this comes along. And right now, I can't even imagine telling my parents.'

I sigh, placing a consoling hand on her shoulder. 'You're gonna have to come clean soon, you know.'

She blows out a breath, as if she's been holding it since she found out she was pregnant. 'I know. I just... I need a plan when I tell them. Not to be totally in the dark when it comes to how my life is going to pan out.'

'And have you thought about what you want to do?' I ask, trying not to sound too overly worried.

She shrugs. 'The thing is that it's all dependent on whether my parents want to help me. They could throw me out for all I know, and then I'm homeless with a baby on the way.'

I roll my eyes. 'Anna, I'm not going to watch you go homeless. I'll help in any way I can.'

'Really? Do you have a place of your own?' she asks, with hopeful eyes.

'Err... no,' I admit bashfully. 'I did, but now I'm back at my mum and dads.'

'Oh.' She's obviously worried that the grown woman

giving her advice is living back with her parents in her thirties. Not exactly a role model to aspire to.

'Look, I realise my life hardly sounds like the best in the world. And it isn't, but that doesn't mean you should lose heart.'

'Okay.' She doesn't seem convinced.

'I'll drop you home and I think you should have a long think about how you're going to tell them.'

'Great,' she snorts sarcastically. 'Can't wait.'

Chapter 11

Wednesday 24th Jan

Anna's been avoiding me all rehearsal. I know it's because she clearly hasn't told her parents and obviously has no idea how she's going to do it. I want to tell her that I understand though. It can't be easy.

I asked Hartley where the programmes were, and he looked back at me blankly, so I've volunteered to go through it with him after the kids leave. As the last teenager escapes out the door we settle down on the stage floor with his laptop.

'I'm no good at this stuff,' he whines, hitting the computer when he can't seem to format anything how he wants.

'Alright, hulk,' I chuckle. 'Hand it over before you break the thing.'

I grab the laptop and press a few buttons I'm well used to using. 'Right, let's plan out the sequence and write down any songs the audience are encouraged to sing along to.'

'Right,' he nods, pressing the palms of his hands to his eyes. 'Thank God you're here. Heather used to handle all this for me.'

'That's what I'm here for,' I smile. I can't help but be flattered. It's nice to feel useful.

'Are you hungry? I could murder a pizza.'

My stomach grumbles right on cue. 'Ah, probably look weird if I say I'm alright now, wouldn't it?'

'Yep,' he snorts. 'I'll order one.'

He takes his phone and opens the app, taking my order.

'I'll go stand outside,' he says, standing up. 'Make sure they don't drive past us.'

'Yeah, yeah,' I joke playfully, 'any excuse to get away with not doing more of this.'

I throw myself into it, with a lot to get through. Before it even feels like a minute has gone by he's walking back in with pizza boxes stacked on top of each other and a bottle of wine.

'Wine?' I grin. 'What kind of pizza place do you order from? Because I clearly need their number.'

He chuckles. 'I thought I'd treat us. Thank you for staying late to do this. I'm so sorry to keep you from your life.'

I snort, taking the boxes off him and starting to open them. 'What life? All I'd be doing is sitting at home watching the soaps.'

He grins. 'So really I'm saving you.'

I grab a slice of pizza. 'Whatever helps you sleep at night.' I bite into the pizza. Mmm! What is it about food tasting the best when you're ravenous? Your stomach is just so grateful you're munching down on something.

'No glasses I'm afraid, so we're gonna have to drink out of the bottle,' he says, taking a swig.

I laugh. 'Luckily for you that's my favourite way to drink it. That or a straw,' I joke, taking the bottle and having a large swig. Ah, everything is better with wine.

We stuff our faces with the pizza, garlic bread, and potato wedges. By the time it's all finished I'm stuffed to bursting and we've drained the bottle of wine. Whoops. That went quick.

'The good news is that I'm all done with this programme. All you have to do is print it in the morning.'

'You are a bloody angel.'

I feel my cheeks blushing. 'It's no big deal.' I close the pizza lid to stop my hands shaking at the way he's suddenly got serious.

He places his hand on top of mine, the warmth of it shocking me. It's so smooth and tanned. I look up into his forest-green eyes—so intense they seem to hold me in place—struggling to keep my emotions in check.

A connection buzzes between us, as if palpable in the air. I find myself leaning a millimetre towards him. It's enough for me to cringe inwardly. What the hell am I doing? I watch too many Hallmark movies.

Only, well... then he moves ever so slightly towards me. It must only be a couple of centimetres but it's enough to find myself staring at his lips and moving closer to them, like a moth to a flame. I lick my own, my heart rate racing erratically. So loud I'm worried he'll hear it.

Mind you, now that I look at his chest, it seems to be heaving up and down just as badly. I could move myself a few more inches and our lips would be touching. We'd be kissing. I'd be letting go of all this locked up frustration. Finally find out how he tastes. But I'd be kissing someone else's fiancé.

I pull back just in time. What the hell am I doing?

'Sorry,' I utter, staring back at him, with my mouth open.

He stares back at me, as if shocked himself. 'No, I'm sorry.'

I stand up. 'It's fine.' I grab my coat and bag and run.

Thursday 25th January

I barely slept all last night. What the hell is going on with me? I abhor cheating and there I was, mouth ripe and ready to be kissed like some wanton little whore. The fact is that he's engaged. Yeah, he might have said he doesn't want to be, but he hasn't broken it off with her. I'm still planning their wedding.

When I did finally fall asleep, I only managed forty minutes before being woken up by a text from Mia. I really need to remember to place it on silent. I look at the time and see it's already seven thirty in the morning.

'Meeting you for lunch today with Kelly. 1pm at Pietro's Cafe. Already cleared it with Hugh so don't go thinking you can use work as an excuse.'

Damn these bitches. I'm so tired I can just about stomach dragging myself into work for some emails, let alone talk to people. But I know them too well. They won't let me get out of it, even if I crashed on the way and broke my collarbone. They'd still be skyping me from my hospital bed, wanting to find out all the goss.

So, I drag myself out of bed, and throw myself in the shower while talking myself out of the benefits of drowning. I deliberately wear something bright as if it will wake me up. I pick my jazzy purple top and team it with a hot pink pencil skirt.

By the time I'm dragging my tired legs into Pietro's cafe I've had four coffees and I'm feeling buzzed. But behind that I'm still tired and distracted. I just have to get through today. One day at a time.

The girls are already sat there waiting for me.

'Hey, bitch,' Mia says, standing to give me a hug.

Kelly waves excitedly from the table. I sit down and give her a side hug.

'So, what's up ladies?' I ask as soon as I've ordered my extra-large coffee from the waitress.

They exchange a quick glance.

Kelly smiles at me warily. 'We were just wondering how you've taken the news of Flo's baby?'

Oh, now I see the sudden urgency. Flo obviously called them and told them to look out for my imminent breakdown.

I sigh to let them know how ridiculous they're being. 'I'm seriously fine, guys. There really is no need to worry.'

'You're sure?' Mia checks, eyeing me up suspiciously. 'Because you know you can tell us and we won't go back and tell Flo, right?'

'That's sweet of you, but I'm happy for them. I mean, yeah, do I wish I had a baby of my own? Of course.' They nod sympathetically. 'Do I wish I had a man of my own to lean on?' Why is it my throat is suddenly feeling tight with emotion? 'Of course,' I agree, my voice breaking slightly.

What the hell is wrong with me?

'Oh, hun,' Kelly says, moving her chair closer. 'Let it all out.'

A traitorous tear falls down my cheek. Ugh, I despise crying, let alone in public.

'I seriously don't know why I'm even crying.' I try to

laugh, but it comes out as more of a sob.

A couple on the table across from us turn to stare at me. Ugh, I'm drawing attention.

'Oh, love,' Mia says, reaching her hand across the table and settling it above mine. 'Want me to take your mind off it?'

I sniff. 'Yes please.'

'Well, Troy's dick is magnificent.'

Kelly spits out her coffee, covering the table in her spray. What the hell?

'Jesus, Kelly! Mia shrieks. 'You almost got my purse.' She picks up her bag and shakes off the slight coffee drops from the leather bag.

'To be fair,' I laugh, 'you did just talk about dick over lunch.'

She snorts. 'Don't make out like it's the first time we've discussed it. And anyway, I was trying to take your mind off things.' She widens her arms and points inwards at herself. 'Trying to be a good friend here.'

'Have you finally slept with him?' Kelly asks, eyes wide and leaning forward. I take the tissue she offers me.

'No,' Mia shrugs, as if she didn't just tell us his dick was magnificent.

'Then how the hell have you seen his dick?' I shout in frustration.

Every single person in the restaurant seems to stop talking at once and turns to stare at me. Oh crap. Well, if I

hadn't drawn attention to myself from crying then I've definitely done it now.

Mia bursts out laughing. 'That could seriously only happen to you!'

We wait until people start to go back to their own conversations, the nosy bastards, and then Kelly starts interrogating her.

'What the hell do you mean? You've seen his peen but haven't slept with him?' she whisper-hisses.

Mia's eyes light up with humour. 'I mean that he crashed at mine the other night and I saw it.'

'Sorry, I need more details,' I demand. 'Did he sleep in your bed? Was he naked? Were you naked?'

'Alright, calm down, Cilla.' She rolls her eyes. 'He was having a night out down the road and I just offered rather than him having to get a cab. He slept on the sofa and he wore his boxer shorts. But...' She smiles coyly, her eyes alight with wickedness.

'But what?' Kelly demands, practically climbing over the table to shake her shoulders.

'Well, they were quite tight, and I basically saw everything. All of his meat and two veg and let me tell you, he is *very* well endowed.'

Kelly snorts a laugh. 'It's true what they say about black men, you know.' She wiggles her eyebrows suggestively.

'Oh please,' Mia snorts with a roll of her eyes. 'What

are you basing that on? Your one ex-boyfriend that happened to be black?'

'Black and with a massive cock,' she answers defensively.

'I doubt that's enough to judge a whole race's penis size though,' I counter.

'Whatever,' she snorts, folding her arms across her chest. 'I know I'm right.'

Mia shrugs. 'I wouldn't know. To be honest, he's the first black guy that I've ever fancied. Is that weird? Do you think I'm secretly racist?'

I burst out laughing. 'Mia, if you were racist you wouldn't want to be anywhere near the dude, let alone be thinking about his dick.'

She grins dreamily. 'And my, what a dick it is.'

'You getting thirsty for it?' Kelly asks with a laugh. 'Come on, spill the tea, girl.'

I roll my eyes. 'Kelly, you need to stop watching those American sitcoms. You're starting to talk weird.'

She scoffs. 'Whatever.' She turns back to Mia. 'So, come on. You're hot for this guy. What the hell is stopping you?

She sighs wearily. 'Because I've never had a male friend before.'

'Never?' I shriek. 'What, even back at school?'

She shakes her head. 'No, never. I always ended up ruining it by sleeping with them.'

'Ah,' me and Kelly both nod at the same time.

'So, you're scared you're going to fuck it up by sleeping with him?'

'Exactly,' she nods, twisting her purple hair around her finger. 'It's just so good right now with us being mates. I don't want it all to go down the shitter.'

I smile. 'But what if it doesn't go down the shitter? What if it becomes the best relationship you've ever had?'

She blushes. Actually blushes. I've never seen Mia blush. Ever.

'It's all irrelevant anyway. We've both said there's no point in doing anything until we're both ready to settle down and I'm pretty sure he still has a few more oats to sew.'

'Oats to sew?' Kelly shrieks. 'Have you turned into an eighty-year-old woman overnight?'

She bursts out laughing. 'I don't know what's happening with me anymore. Look, let's go out tomorrow night. Get me drunk so we can forget about it?'

'I've got the play,' I muse out loud.

'Play?' Kelly asks. 'What the hell are you talking about?'

I forgot I haven't told them about helping Hartley out.

'Oh, Hugh decided to volunteer me for teaching duty at his cousin Clara's, fiancé's school.'

I see them putting that together in their heads.

'He's a drama teacher. So, I'm helping with the school play. It's tomorrow.'

They exchange a glance.

'Why are you blushing so hard?' Mia asks me, her lip quirking with a grin.

'Am I?' I touch my cheeks to feel if they're heated. 'I don't know why I would be.'

'Do you fancy someone at the school or something?' Kelly asks taking a sip of her coffee. 'You don't fancy one of their teenagers, do you? I know they look older these days, but you can still go to prison for that shit.'

I scoff a laugh. 'As if! I'm no paedo.'

The restaurant goes quiet again. Horrified faces stare back at me. Why does this keep happening?

'So, who is it you fancy then?' Mia asks, leaning in with interest.

'No one.' Now I can feel myself blushing. I must be beetroot by now.

She licks her lips, as if sensing the gossip. 'I know you; those blushes tell me you like someone.'

'It's not the groom is it?' Kelly asks with a snort of a laugh.

I stare down into my coffee, unable to meet their judging gazes.

'Holy shit balls!' Mia shrieks. 'It is. You fancy the groom?'

'Ssh!' I hiss, looking around at the restaurant. We can never come here again. 'Of course not.'

'I call bullshit,' Mia laughs. 'But whatever. This

confirms it. As soon as the play is over we're going out. And we're going to drink our feelings away.'

'Yes!' Kelly says with a punch to the air. 'Let's get lit!'

'No more American TV for you!' I screech.

Friday 26th January

By the time I get to the school the next afternoon I've had three phone calls from Clara. The first was asking if we could also arrange penguins to be there. The second was if we could accommodate a ten-tier cake, and the third was if I knew of any good diet pills. I mean, really? The woman is bloody tiny already. I'm dreading seeing her here later. And kind of secretly wishing she orders some dodgy ones online that give her the shits.

Thank goodness I came to help out though. Every student is so bloody nervous, buzzing around, forgetting what costume they should be wearing. Luckily, due to my costume filing system I'm able to pull them together and sort them out.

Hartley comes in looking completely frazzled, his hair bedraggled.

'You okay?' I ask carefully, scared he's going to snap at me.

'Yeah, just stressed the fuck out. Emily's ill so we've got Jamie filling in. Do you think we could give him a fake pair of boobs, so he looks more female?'

I smile. Nothing a pair of rolled up socks can't fix. That's how I got through high school. 'Don't worry, send him back here and I'll sort him out.'

He sighs, his shoulders finding their way back down from his ears. 'Thanks, Nadine. I don't know what I would have done without you.'

I beam back at him, but quickly remind myself to calm the fuck down. In the words of Chaka Khan, somebody else's guy.

'What time's Clara getting here?' I ask in an attempt to remind myself.

He sighs, his shoulders slumping. 'She just rang and said she has to stay at work for a last-minute meeting.'

Oh, bless him. Poor Hartley. Just when he needs her. He looks like he needs a hug and the urge to do it myself is so overpowering I have to force my hands to stay at my sides.

'Don't worry, the show must go on,' I say, attempting to be cheery.

'Yeah, but will it be any good?' he asks, his eyes hopeful.

I hold him by his biceps and give him a little shake. It's hard to move him when he's such a bloody tree.

'You're going to be fine. The play will be fab. Just take a deep breath and let's get on with it.'

He takes a deep inhale of breath, nods and walks out.

I shouldn't be the one doing this. It should be Clara. No wonder he doesn't want to marry her.

Three hours later and the play has come to an end. I can't believe we managed to pull it off. All went smoothly. Well, all apart from one of Jamie's rolled up socks falling out, which got a laugh from the audience.

I'm just picking up the last discarded costume from the floor when Hartley comes in holding an open bottle of Prosecco.

'We did it!' he says, his face lit up in a mix of relief and happiness.

He's so cute. I smile back at him, feeling strangely proud myself. I can't believe we pulled it off. 'It all went well, didn't it?'

'Thank God. I didn't let on, but I was a lot more nervous than you'd think.'

I snort a laugh. Did he seriously think he was hiding it well? 'Yeah, I kind of twigged on.'

'Didn't hide it as well as I thought, then, huh?' He chuckles, his eyes sparkling in the light.

'Not quite.'

'Anyway,' he suddenly seems apprehensive, pushing the hair from his face, 'a crowd of us are going to grab a drink at The Slug and Dog. Do you want to join us?'

I feel that same strong pull towards him, like a magnet,

so strong it's hard to resist. So, I quickly decide it's a bad idea.

'Thanks, but I'm already going out.'

He smiles sadly. 'Oh really? Date is it?'

I scoff. 'Nope. Night out with the girls.'

'Have a quick celebratory drink with me?' He pulls out two plastic cups from his back pocket and starts pouring the Prosecco. 'It's not the proper stuff I'm afraid. Our teacher budgets don't stretch very far.'

He hands over my cup. I take it shyly, self-consciously tucking a strand of hair behind my ear. Luckily for him I prefer Prosecco. He raises his cup at me. I raise mine to his, his eyes locking with mine. 'Cheers.'

'Cheers.'

An awkward silence descends on the room as we both drink from our cups. This is awful. I need to get out of here. I can't stand the tension, which I'm pretty sure is just in my head.

I stand up and make to leave. 'I should go.'

'Wait!' he calls, forcing me to turn around to face him, eyes raised in question.

He puts one of his hands in his trouser pockets. 'The school's having a float competition tomorrow. Will you come?'

I bite my lip. I should be staying well away from this man, not spending more time with him.

'I'm not sure,' I falter, arguing with my inner slut that

I must leave him alone. 'I mean, I never normally get this involved with my wedding couples.'

He smiles, his eyes locked onto mine. 'I know.' He clears his throat, shaking his head as if to pull himself together. 'It's just that the students seem to love you and it would be a great way to thank you for everything you've done. There will be free cakes and tea.'

I can't help but crack a smile at him trying to break the atmosphere. How can someone so sexy also be so adorable?

'Free cakes and tea? Why the hell didn't you lead with that?' I chuckle. 'Of course, I'll be there.'

He smiles, his eyes sparkling. 'Great.' It's as if they're daring me to come for him. I want to so much it scares me right now.

I grab my bag. 'Gotta go!'

I really shouldn't be looking forward to this, but I am. And I'm not sure what kind of person that makes me. I'm really not sure where my morals are anymore.

Chapter 12

Saturday 27th January

Why I promised to come today when I knew I was going out with the girls, I'll never know. They were throwing shots down my throat and forcing me to dance on the bar until two am when Mia called Troy and he magically appeared to drop us home. Those two are so bloody cosy. I really do wonder if she's lying to us and is shagging him after all. Why else would he care so much? Apparently, he just wanted to make sure we got home safe. Unless he's really that sweet. My trust in men is currently at an all time low.

They might be teenagers but watching the school kids dressed in their play outfits waving from their float has me almost tearing up, staring on emotionally like I'm watching my old class of five-year-olds.

I suppose in a way they are, they were once little kids

and now they're growing into little people. It's scary to think about how quickly it happens. Then I think of Belle. She'd be three years old now. I force down the pain threatening to consume me. I'm too hungover to allow myself to get upset right now. Better to lock it back up.

Their float is decorated in the school colours of blue and yellow. Hobbycraft must be empty because it looks like all the crepe paper in the world has been used.

Other schools pass by with their floats too. They might only be going ten miles an hour, but they're all basically stood on the back of a truck with not a seatbelt in sight. Health and safety would be all over this. You'd think with a school they'd have to stick to certain rules. I suppose when there's the promise of a winner's ribbon it's easy to forget.

Hartley looks amazing on it, chatting away and laughing with his students. They really love him and who can blame them? I've only known him a few weeks and I feel almost obsessed with him.

I keep looking around for Clara but she's nowhere to be seen. I don't get it; it's a Saturday. She can't be working on a Saturday, can she? Its four pm and even I've managed to get someone to cover me for the rest of the wedding at The Duck and Goose. Thank God, I have staff I can rely on.

They're just doing their final loop when suddenly their float starts gaining speed. Why the hell are they going so fast? If they keep this up they're going to veer right into the other oncoming float. I watch in horror; they are.

Murmurs of concern go through the crowd, some parents screaming. The float just about scrapes past the other float, but heads straight towards the corner shop. Shit!

The whole crowd starts running towards it, but it's too late. We watch in horror as it smashes into the corner of it, everyone being slung forward. I'm running before I can register the shock. Holy crap. Are they okay? Anna's on that float. The baby!

By the time I get to it there's a crowd of people already surrounding it. Paramedics from the first aid tent are trying to help everyone. The driver is slumped over the wheel. He must have had a heart attack or something.

I have to find Anna and Hartley. Make sure they're okay.

I push past everyone's terrified parents and rush to the front. I can't see Hartley but notice Anna jump off the back.

I rush to her. 'Anna! Are you okay?'

'Yeah,' she says, out of breath, her eyes still startled. 'I'm okay.'

'You need to be checked out by the paramedic anyway.' I grab a passing one. 'Excuse me, but she needs to be checked immediately.'

The paramedic quickly looks her over, clearly confused as she doesn't have any clear injuries.

'I'm sorry, madam, but we're dealing with everyone by the severity of their injuries. She looks unharmed.'

My patience is running thin. What if something happens to the baby? I can't let that happen because some stupid paramedic refused to see her.

'But you don't get it. She's pregnant.'

Anna touches my arm. I turn to see her frozen in alarm, her big doe eyes wider than normal. She literally looks like Bambi caught in the headlights.

'Anna.'

We both turn. I see who I was earlier introduced to as the headmaster. Oh no, did he hear me?

'I hope to God I didn't hear that right, Miss Giordano.'

'Err...'

His face is murderous. I don't even go to this school and I think I may have just peed my pants.

'Get yourself checked out and then I want to speak to you back at the school.' He turns and storms off.

What the hell have I done?

Anna's eyes quickly fill with tears. 'What am I going to do?'

'I'm so sorry, Anna! I was just worried about you.'

'Excuse me, Miss,' the paramedic says to her, 'but we should check you over. If you'd follow me.'

'It's fine,' Anna says to me on a heavy sigh. 'They were going to find out eventually. It was inevitable.' She turns and walks away with the paramedic, her shoulders slumped.

I don't have the luxury of time to feel bad. I have to find Hartley and make sure he's okay. I walk around the float and find him helping students down safely. When he turns I see he has a gash on his head which is slowly dripping blood down past his eye.

'Hartley!' I shout, running towards him. I throw myself against his chest, so pleased he's okay. I quickly realise how inappropriate and over the top I'm being. I pull back and gesture to his head. 'You need to come to the first aid tent.'

'I'm fine,' he shrugs. 'I'm needed here.'

'No,' I insist, tugging on his arm like a petulant child. 'There's enough people here to help. You need looking at.'

He sighs heavily, rolling his eyes. 'Fine.'

I drag him by the arm towards the first aid tent. I pull him into it and point to a paramedic fiddling with her thumbs. Jesus, has she not heard there's been a major crash?

'Help. He hit his head,' I explain.

She thankfully jumps into action straightaway, asking all about it.

'I'm afraid you're going to have to have some stitches. You can go to the hospital or I can just do them quickly now?'

He looks to me, then back at her. 'Just do them now.'

'Okay.'

'But...' he turns to me with a pretend pout. 'You'll have to hold my hand.'

I smile and roll my eyes. 'Fine,' I snap, pretending to

be put out.

I sit down across from him and let his large warm hand engulf mine. It feels so nice I have to stop myself from openly moaning like a complete nutcase.

Is it me or does he suddenly not look so confident? Was his joke hiding some truth behind it? Is he scared?

The paramedic starts prepping it and his grip tightens slightly.

'Take my mind off it, will you,' he says quickly, averting his gaze to anywhere but at the paramedic.

'Okay, what do you want me to do?' I literally have no party tricks I can pull out of the bag. I really wish I could juggle right now.

'Talk to me about something.'

Christ, the pressure. It's like my mind has gone blank with panic.

'Err... I like bananas.' He raises his eyebrows at me, amusement dancing in his eyes. 'I... err... I like them a lot. I have them in my morning porridge and I love banana bread. Florence makes the best banana bread ever. I've tried to make it myself, but I have to let the bananas go really ripe and I've always eaten them by then. And I mean, I once ate so many of them that I was constipated for three days. So now I have to ration myself to one a day.'

He stares back at me, eyes wide with alarmed amusement.

'You really are nuts, aren't you?'

'No,' I say defiantly. 'You're the one that wanted me to talk to you. I could quite happily go off home and leave you here, but you wanted me to talk.'

'Not about bananas.'

'Well, I'm *sorry* if I don't have a suitable, sophisticated subject up my sleeve, ready to whip out when someone I know gets a head injury.'

He squeezes my hand, as if to try to calm me down. 'I'm sorry.'

I smile back, instantly forgiving him.

'It's just I didn't think you'd tell me about being constipated.'

I burst out laughing. Blimey, what am I like? I have zero class.

'All done,' the paramedic says with a smile. I'd forgotten she was here for a minute. 'But I do need you to keep a close eye on him for the next twenty-four hours. If he seems overly sleepy or complains of a bad headache contact a doctor immediately.'

I stare back at her. 'Oh, I'll tell his fiancée.' I look shyly back at him.

'Oh', she says taken aback. 'I'm sorry, I just assumed you two were together.'

Hartley takes his hand from mine in a hurry. 'No, we're just friends,' he explains, the air suddenly thick with cringe-worthy tension.

'Right, well will your fiancée be with you for the next

twenty-four hours?'

'I'm fine,' he insists with a nod.

She smiles back sternly. 'I didn't ask that. I asked if she was going to be with you.' Ooh, get this feisty bitch.

He sighs heavily. 'No. She's away with work for the weekend.'

Jesus, that woman is never home.

'Ah,' She looks back at him with concern. 'Could you stay with your parents?' she asks, cleaning up her kit.

He shrugs. 'Nope. Both pushing up daisies.'

Pushing up daisies? Oh, he means they're dead. That's so sad. I'm so close to my parents. I can't imagine them not being around.

'What about some friends?' I ask intrigued as to who's in his inner circle.

'They're all away in Prague for a stag do. I didn't go because of today.'

Wow, that's dedication for you.

'You could...' I start.

'What?' he asks eagerly, chewing on his lip.

Crap. Why did I open my stupid mouth? 'I suppose you could always come back to mine.' Does that sound slutty? I'm just trying to make sure he doesn't drop down dead.

'It sounds like the only option,' the paramedic agrees with a nod.

'But...' How do I tell him I still live with my parents?

This is awkward.

'What's wrong?' he asks, placing his warm hand over mine. He really needs to stop doing that unless he wants me to face fuck him.

I feel my cheeks redden. 'It's just that I live with my parents. Don't get me wrong, they'd be fine with you staying, but it's pretty embarrassing.'

'No, it's not,' he says with a shake of his head.

'I did move out; it's just that I ended up moving back in,' I clarify, trying to sound less of a thirty-two-year-old loser.

'Don't worry. You don't have to explain yourself. I honestly don't care.'

He doesn't look embarrassed to know me, which is sometimes the reaction I get.

'Great,' the paramedic nods. She hands over a list of symptoms for me to look out for and dismisses us.

When we walk out of the tent we find that most people are off listening to the winners being announced at the other side of the green. I suddenly remember Anna.

'Oh God, Hartley, I really dropped Anna in it earlier.'

He frowns. 'With who?'

'Your headmaster overheard me telling the paramedic she was pregnant.'

He smiles sadly, placing his hand on my shoulder. 'Hey, don't beat yourself up. You were only concerned for her.'

'I just couldn't bear for something to happen to the baby just because she was too embarrassed to tell them.'

He nods seriously. 'You did the right thing.'

His hand squeezes my shoulder. It's so brief, its over before a second passes, but it leaves a spark, a tingling feeling travelling all the way down my arm.

'You're a nice person. A great person actually.' He looks into my eyes and it's as if time sits still, a current passing between us that only we can feel.

Or maybe it's just me and he feels nothing.

I force myself out of it with a shake of the head and gesture towards my car. We walk together towards it, tension still thick around us. I have no idea why. I'm pretty sure I'm the only one crushing here.

I go to unlock my car when he takes my hand. I look down at our intertwined fingers in disbelief. He yanks me, pulling me towards a nearby alleyway. What the hell is he doing?

He slams me hard against the wall, so hard that I cower away from him. I stare up at him in fear, but instead of seeing the expected anger looming in his forest-green eyes, I see something else I can't put my finger on.

His hand cups my jaw. His eyes, alight with the emotion I can now pinpoint as lust, stare at me only for a split-second before he crushes his lips against mine. Those delicious lips: plump, soft and with the slight taste of mint.

He pushes his tongue into my mouth, caressing mine

urgently. It's hot as hell. Before I know what I'm doing I have my hands around his neck and I'm pulling at his hair, feeling so wild and wanton that I could rip it out just to have my claim over him.

His hands travel down my neck, underneath my hair, slowly over my spine until they're on my arse. He pushes me into his hardness. Wow, someone's a big boy. I gasp in surprise.

Wait, what the hell am I doing? This guy is engaged to be married! Married at my wedding venue. I've lost my mind!

I push him off with all my might, using every last shred of self-control. It takes him a while to realise and when he does he only pulls his body off me, his forehead tilting against mine.

His eyes stare intently at me. 'I'm sorry,' he says, out of breath.

My chest heaves up and down, my body short of breath and my mind whirling.

'You're engaged,' is all I can answer back.

He sighs heavily, as if the weight of the world is on his shoulders. 'I just... I couldn't stop myself.'

I peel away from underneath him and escape under his arm.

'Well you're going to have to. I'm not that kind of woman.' But my God, how I want to be.

He turns towards me, dragging his hand through his

hair. 'Trust me, I know that. That's half of the appeal.'

I frown back at him. 'What, because I'm some feeble woman who's easy to manipulate?' I cross my arms over my chest. What an arsehole.

HIs eyes widen. 'No! Of course not. It's just that you're so different to Clara. You're not the type of girl to attempt breaking up a couple.'

Hearing her name out loud feels like I've taken a bullet. That's obviously why he thinks he fancies me. He's scared of getting married and he's deliberately looking for someone the exact opposite of Clara. You couldn't get more opposite than me.

'Look, I get it,' I say with a nod, avoiding his penetrating gaze. 'You're having cold feet and you're looking for an excuse to get out of it. But I'm not it.'

He takes a deep breath, as if to try to shake himself out of it. 'It's not that.'

'Look, whatever it is, let's just try to forget it happened, okay?'

He looks at me intently, so intently I fear I'll set on fire. 'Fine.'

I swallow down the lump in my throat, desperate not to burst into tears right here.

'Okay, come on.'

He furrows his brows. 'Come on where?'

'My house,' I answer, turning to walk back towards the car.

'You still want me around?' he asks, slowly following me.

I nod. 'As long as you promise not to jump me,' I say with a giggle. 'I promised to look after you and I don't break a promise.

He smiles, glad I've lightened the mood. 'Okay. I promise.'

Chapter 13

The ride back home is a little awkward to say the least. Every time I think of his lips on mine I almost crash the car.

'So how long have you lived back at your parents?' he asks, clearly in an attempt to break the tense atmosphere.

'About three years now.' I sound like such a loser.

'What made you move back? London rent prices?'

If only he knew the truth. That would really scare the crap out of him.

I nod instead. 'Something like that.' I pull into my street and parallel park like a pro.

'Wow, woman, you can park.' he says, in shocked admiration.

'Excuse me?' I ask in amusement. Did he think I wouldn't be able to just because I'm a woman?

'I'm used to women who can't drive, but you just swung

in that spot like it was no big deal.'

I smile at the compliment. 'I've lived here my whole life. I'm just used to it. Come on.'

He follows me towards the small terrace house we live in. It's not much, but its home. Florence's mum still lives next door with her partner Joan.

'Mum!' I call as soon as I open the door, the heat welcoming me back. I can already feel myself thawing.

'In here, love,' she shouts back from the kitchen.

I follow the voice. 'Don't freak out, but I brought someone back.'

She turns around from the oven, her face wrinkled in horror. You see my mum likes to be prepared for guests. Have her hair done and lipstick on. Right now, she's in her pyjamas with her hair in a pineapple on top of her head.

'Tell me you're joking,' she shrieks.

Hartley walks slowly into the kitchen. 'I'm afraid she isn't,' he says, with an awkward wave.

'Oh, what on earth's happened to your head?' she asks, rushing over for a closer inspection. Mum likes to think she's a proper nurse occasionally, not just a dental one. Since she took that first aid course she acts like she has a PhD.

'Our float crashed,' he explains with an eye roll. 'Bit of a drama, but I'm fine.'

She turns back to me, her eyes creased in confusion.

'He was on a school float,' I explain. 'For a parade.

He's a teacher.'

'Oh,' she says, a wide smile on her face as she takes in the rest of Hartley's handsome features. Obviously assessing him as husband material for me. She has no idea he's someone else's.

Then I remember I haven't even introduced him properly.

'Sorry, Mum, this is Hartley.'

'Lovely to meet you, Hartley,' she says with a broad smile, before engulfing him in a hug. My family are huggers. Normal people are sometimes taken aback by all of the affection.

'Lovely to meet you too,' he says with a friendly smile. 'Your daughter was kind enough to offer to look after me overnight, make sure I don't pass out from concussion. But I'd totally understand if you'd prefer I go home.'

'I won't hear of it!' she insists, slapping him away. 'I've just put an apple pie in the oven so it's perfect timing. Have you had any dinner?'

He shrugs. 'I had a sandwich earlier, so I'm fine, thanks.'

She scoffs, as if the idea of a sandwich is ridiculous for such a big strapping man like him.

'Well then you must be starving! Let me make you both some beans on toast.'

He continues to charm the pants off my mum all evening. I can see her getting excited and giving me the occasional look which I can read means *'he's a keeper!'* The poor thing thinks I've brought a man home for her to check out. She has no idea. But hey, while she's thinking that at least I can try to forget how inappropriate all of this is.

We watch TV with just a lamp on in the corner. I can feel myself dropping off, the drama of today mixed with my full belly exhausting me. Without overthinking it I grab a cushion, place it in his lap and lie my head down onto it. He doesn't seem to react, so I let the warmth of his body wrap around me like a blanket.

♡♡♡

When I open my eyes, I find I'm still in the same place I fell asleep, snuggled on Hartley's lap. I can feel the warmth of his arm over my back. The lights are all out apart from the glow of the TV, some random all-night bingo programme on.

I sit up to see Hartley's head thrown back; he's snoring his head off. It makes me giggle. I cover my mouth with my hand so as not to wake him, but it's too late. He stirs, one eye opening first, then the other.

He doesn't say anything, just stares at me. He's such a sexy fucker, those eyes shining down at me in the barely lit room. The darkness makes me feel bold. Call it my dream-like state or the fact that I'm already so close to him, but I find myself lifting my bottom and swinging my leg over to straddle him. He watches me, his eyes predatory, his mouth popping open slightly. His breath is coming out in heavy pants.

I want him so much I ache all the way from my lips that want to connect with his again, to my knickers which are soaking wet with need. But I can't do this. I shouldn't do this. He's taken. Why have I always got such terrible taste in men?

He cups my face in both his hands and pulls me to him slowly, watching me intently the whole time. As if waiting for me to back out, to say no. Which I should really do. But I don't, the magnetic force between us too strong and my resolve too weak.

Instead I lean in and let my lips connect with his. I kiss him slowly and deeply, pouring all my unsaid emotions into it. I let him know in our kiss how long I've wanted to do this, how much I've held myself back, even the guilt I'm already feeling.

I attempt to memorise the feel of his lips on mine, savour the taste of his tongue and the sensations he's causing as one hand tangles into my hair. God, don't touch my hair. Game over. This bitch has been conquered.

We lose ourselves in the kiss, tangling our bodies against each other, the warmth of his body melting my last shred of resistance.

He stops suddenly, pulling back to grin at me, his eyes fuelled with lust. His hands find my hips, moving me to one side, as if I weigh the same as a feather. Wait, is he moving me to stop? My stomach flips at the rejection, my heart straining against my chest, as if it wants to jump out and personally urge me to carry on kissing him.

He stands but surprises me when he takes my hand. I stand up and let him lead me upstairs. Oh my God. We're really going to do this.

This is wrong. So wrong.

I ignore that niggling voice in my head and decide to do something completely selfish for once. Just to listen to my body and let it decide. I can deal with the consequences tomorrow.

I'm careful to creep slowly on the floorboards. The last thing I want is to wake up Mum, or myself, from this dream where I get to live in the moment and only care about myself.

When we get to the top of the stairs the bathroom door opens and out walks Dad. Shit, I had no idea he'd even got back from work. I freeze, my mouth hanging open, completely caught red-handed.

'Nadine,' he gasps, looking down at our interlinked fingers.

'Dad.'

'Mr Valentine,' Dad says to Hartley. Wait, he knows him?

'Hi,' Hartley says, immediately dropping my hand like it's on fire.

'How do you two know each other?' I ask, desperate to

know. It's still dimly lit up here, only the moonlight shining through the hallway window, but it's enough to see that the colour from Hartley's face has drained away.

'Mr Blumenkrantz brought him round to meet us the other day.'

Dad knows Clara's dad?

'How do you know Mr Blumenkrantz?'

He rolls his eyes, his jaw tight with barely concealed outrage. 'Nadine, he owns the company. I'm sure I've mentioned that before.'

I shake my head. I really need to start listening to him when he rambles on.

Dad looks pointedly at Hartley, assessing him up and down. 'How's your *fiancée*, Mr Valentine?'

Well, fuck. I was at least hoping he wouldn't know that tiny bit of information. Give me something to cling onto.

Hartley discreetly moves further away from me. 'Yeah, she's good, thanks.' He turns to me, swallowing hard, the fear of God in his eyes. 'Thanks for offering to keep an eye on me, but I'm pretty sure I'd have shown signs of concussion by now. I should go.'

He turns and bolts down the stairs and out of the door.

Dad looks back at me, eyes raised as if waiting for an explanation. He doesn't need to say anything. I feel awful enough. He turns and walks into his bedroom leaving me feeling like the other slutty woman that I am.

Why is it the one man who seems to have the key to

unlock my heart already belongs to another?

186

Chapter 14

Sunday 28th January

I still can't believe I was so close to sleeping with him. A soon to be married man. What is it about this dude? The minute I get around him I start acting like a wanton whore. He must have some kind of pheromones that make women crazy. I'm sure I'm not alone. Surely every woman that meets him falls at his feet?

Anyway, luckily today I have Sunday lunch with Mia, Kelly and Florence, to take my mind off it. Dad couldn't even look at me over breakfast this morning. I really hope he didn't tell Mum Hartley's engaged. I can't take more judgement. Well warranted, but still.

I've just walked in and sat down in the cosy pub with its open fire when Mia and Kelly start leaning across the table and whispering to me.

'Quick, before Florence gets here,' Mia says in a rush. 'We need to organise a date for her baby shower.'

'It's a bit bloody soon to be organising that isn't it?' I ask, unable to hide my astonishment. She's only ten bloody weeks.

Kelly and Mia exchange a glance. What the hell was that?

'I don't think so,' Kelly says reasonably with a little shrug. 'With the way our diaries are, it's best to get something pencilled in.'

'I suppose,' I shrug, not agreeing but deciding to go along with it to appease them.

I'm not sure Florence would like this idea. She's already worried she's going to copy Felicity's fate and miscarry before the twelve-week mark. If she found out they were steaming ahead with this I know she'd be mad.

'But aren't they a bit American and like tempting fate?' I voice, not being able to help myself. 'I mean, it's still early days.'

Mia looks at me with pity in her eyes. A look I've come to know so well.

'Babe, bad things can happen regardless of a shower.'

I snort aggressively. 'Trust me, if anyone knows, it's me.'

'We know,' Kelly says, a hand on my arm. 'We know this is going to be really tough for you, which is why we're offering to take this completely off your hands and organise everything.'

Ugh. The last thing I want is some stupid sympathy.

'Don't be stupid,' I snap. 'My best friend is having a baby. I told you the other day I'm happy for her. Don't make out I'm not.'

'We're not!' Mia shouts defensively, hands up as if to surrender.

Gah, where is the waiter? I'd be feeling better about this whole thing if I had some garlic bread right now.

'What have I missed?' Florence asks as she walks towards us. She's looking a lot healthier than the last time I saw her. More of a colour in her cheeks that isn't green.

I stand up to hug her. 'Nothing. You're looking well.'

'I've finally stopped puking you mean,' she says on a smile.

How could they think I'd have any bad feelings towards her? Having a baby is a bloody miracle and yes, I'm scared for her, but in a loving way. I don't begrudge her this. Her and Hugh are such a gorgeous couple. I can't wait to hold their little bundle of joy.

We settle into our usual chatter, catching up on some meaningless gossip from our jobs. I'm desperate to tell them about Hartley, unload some of it, but I know they'd judge me and I'd rather not see that in their eyes.

'Troy said the funniest thing the other day,' Mia says, giggling hysterically.

We all look at each other knowingly, then back at her.

'What?' she asks, barely able to conceal a smile.

'You've got it bad,' I laugh. She's never been this goofy over a guy.

'Shut up,' she snaps, still with that goofy grin on her face.

Those two have been pussyfooting around each other for over a year now. It's ridiculous. I mean, look at me. I meet a soon to be married man and within weeks I've almost bedded him. You can't say I'm not efficient.

'Anyway, any news from you?' Mia asks me, obviously desperate to change the subject.

I've considered telling them since I woke up this morning, but I just can't. Yes, a problem shared is a problem halved, but this affects Florence too. If Hugh finds out, he's going to go spare. He could potentially lose everything: his business, his house and his family. All because I can't keep it in my knickers.

'Nothing really. Just working lots.'

I despise lying, but it's for the best. If I tell them, they'll only try to talk me out of it, which is what I've been doing myself.

'Seen much of Mr Valentine?' Florence asks with a cheeky wink.

I glare back at her. Dammit, Flo, why did she have to bring that up?

'Ooh,' Kelly coos leaning in, 'who on earth is Mr Valentine?'

'Yeah,' Mia nods with a devilish grin. 'And are you fucking?'

'No!' I shriek, far too quickly in hindsight. 'Jesus, I'm organising his wedding. Flo's talking crap.'

They all stare back at me, with raised eyebrows, clearly unconvinced.

'Is that why you've gone bright red?' Florence teases, elbowing me in my ribs. I roll my eyes. She can be so juvenile sometimes.

Just then my phone pings with a text. I open up the unknown number and read it.

I need to see you. Meet me please? Hartley x

My stomach does a nervous flip. How did he get my number? He wants to meet me? What the hell could he want to say? He must be embarrassed about last night and want to apologise. Make sure I'm not going to run back to his fiancée and tell her. Not ask me to run away with him. No, obviously, that would be crazy.

'Everything alright?' Flo asks me, attempting to not so discreetly read my phone over my shoulder.

I quickly put it away. 'Fine, but I've actually got to go.'

'Now?' Kelly says in shock. 'We haven't even ordered bloody starters yet.'

I nod furiously, trying to look confident. 'I forgot I was meeting a wedding couple today.'

'On a Sunday? Jesus, you work too much,' Mia says with a sigh.

'I agree,' Flo nods, chewing on her lip, her eyes suspicious. 'I'm gonna have to speak to Hugh about you getting some help.'

Crap. That's the last thing I need. Hugh looking into what I'm doing.

'Honestly, I'm fine,' I insist. 'I enjoy it. You know how I like to keep busy.'

Kelly gives me a sympathetic smile. It makes me suddenly want to cry. It's one thing being sad at this time of year. It's another being reminded of it and getting the pity look from your besties.

I wave my goodbyes and get out of there sharpish, before the pinching at my throat turns into tears, my mascara runs, and I look like I belong in a Kiss video.

$\heartsuit$

He's asked me to come around his, so we can talk properly. I would've made him come around mine, but Mum has today off so I can hardly invite him there. Plus, I don't want to talk about this anywhere in public. The thought of someone overhearing has me feeling sick to my stomach with dread.

So instead I'm checking the number of his flat in his text and taking a deep breath before knocking on the door, having been let in by a neighbour. Brace yourself Nadine. This is going to be embarrassing. Having someone tell you they regret coming onto you. Never an enjoyable experience. At least I know by the time I'm leaving today it'll all be over. I can go back to my normal shitty little life.

He answers the door wearing soft faded jeans and a navy-blue t-shirt that clings to every curve of muscle. Fuck, he's not going to make it easy for me. I avoid his gaze, instead swinging my eye-line to the floor. And he's barefoot. Why is that sexy? I've never been into feet before but damn his are huge and manly.

'Hi,' he says on a swallow, his Adam's apple bobbing up and down erratically.

Well, at least he's jittery about it too. Means I was right about him and he actually does have a heart. Feels bad for leading me on and then shooting me down.

'Hi.' I smile back at him, attempting to ease his nerves. I realise it's ridiculous for me to feel like I need to make him feel better, but it's just how I am.

He moves for me to walk in and I go past him, desperately trying not to inhale his delicious scent. Too late. Damn he smells good.

I sit myself down on the brown leather sofa hoping he sits on the chair across from me. Nope. He sits right down next to me. This is going to be painful.

I force myself to look around the flat so as not to be forced to face him. The whole place is decorated in white, grey and black. Very stereotypical bachelor pad.

'Nadine...'

I can't bear it. Him fumbling over his words, trying to

find a nice way to let me down gently. Better I just take over and get it over with quickly.

'Look, it's okay,' I interrupt. 'I know what you're going to say.'

He frowns. 'You do?'

I nod. 'Of course, I do. I get it. It was a crazy day yesterday, and you were emotional after the crash. It only makes sense that you needed comfort from someone and with Clara being away, I just ended up being a fill in. Don't worry, I get it.'

He glares back at me. 'No actually, you don't get it at all.'

I stare back at him dumbly. Did I piss him off? What the hell could he be talking about?

'Huh?'

He unleashes the full, devastating effect of his eyes on me. There's no option of me looking away. I feel my body start to tremble, the last shred of resistance starting to drip out of my body.

'I don't think yesterday was a mistake at all.'

My mouth drops open of its own accord. I'm so baffled, my brain's in danger of overheating.

'You... don't?'

Am I reading this wrong right now? Imagining the way he keeps glancing down at my lips as if he wants another taste?

'I think it was bound to happen sooner or later,' he

carries on. My mouth practically hits the floor. 'Nadine, I've been attracted to you from the moment we met. Of course, at first, I tried to ignore it, but it's like I feel this insane pull towards you that I can't describe.'

So, he feels it too?

His eyes skim along the contours of my face as if he finds every detail interesting. 'And now I've got to know you for the sweet, caring woman you are. Well, I'm crazy about you.'

'You...' I gulp, begging my tongue to stop quivering long enough to talk. 'You... are?'

He nods, giving me the cutest lazy smile. 'I am.'

'What about Clara?' I can't help but ask. This all results in bullshit if he doesn't plan on leaving her. Not that I should be encouraging him to leave her. Jesus, I'm a bad person. I'm so going to hell.

'I broke up with her earlier today.'

My eyes widen to twice the size. He broke up with her? He's single right now?

'Cheating isn't who I am, Nadine,' he explains, taking my hand. 'I'm disgusted with myself that we did what we did last night while I was still officially engaged, but if I'm honest I haven't been present in that relationship for a long while.'

'Are you doing this just because you met me?'

Because I can't break up a relationship, and a big part of me wonders if I hadn't come along would he have just gone through with marrying her? Eventually learnt to be happy.

He takes my hand. 'Nadine, although I'm falling for you hard right now, this isn't because of you. You've just given me the push I needed, the one I was looking for to get out of an already dead relationship.'

I can't process this. He's broken up with Clara. He's free and single.

Hugh is going to kill me. I try really hard to care, but with him looking at me like I'm the answer to everything right now it's hard to give one iota of a shit.

'So, you're...' I feel ridiculous saying this, 'available?'

He snorts a laugh before pulling me closer to him. 'I'm free as a bird.'

He plants a quick kiss on my lips, a cheery smile on his. I smile back, still in shock, the blood pumping round my body so furiously I'm surprised he can't hear it.

Then his hands are delving into my hair, grasping and pulling me urgently while his lips attack mine, the hunger in them clear. I let him hold me in place and smother me with kisses, giving in to the immense freedom of letting go. Of letting him kiss me and not feel the crushing guilt normally present on my chest.

He trails his fingertips down my arm causing a shiver of excitement to run up my spine. To counteract the cold, heat rises within me setting my heart racing. My blood pumps around my body quickly, my chest restricted from the lack of oxygen.

I force myself to break away from his lips to grab a breath. He uses the opportunity to push my head back and expose my neck to his peppered kisses. He nips my earlobe, causing me to buck against him. Jesus, I've never been an earlobe kind of girl, but I could get used to this.

He untucks my shirt from my jeans and lifts it up over my head. I pull my bra down so it's still covering me, which I realise too late is a ridiculous thing to do, considering we plan on getting naked. I'm assuming so anyway.

He's unhooked my bra and is pulling it down my arms before I have a chance to feel anymore self-conscious. I still have tiny silver stretch marks on the sides of my boobs from when I was pregnant. It's weird how my stomach got away with it, but my boobs just exploded one night. Thanks to that I'm left with my stretchies. I've never been bothered about them before, but then I haven't been naked with anyone else since me and Joshua broke up. Now I'm suddenly aware of how repulsed a person could find them.

But he doesn't even seem to notice. He's too busy kissing me again, caressing them gently. He moves his kisses back down my neck until he's at my breasts. I wait for the sharp intake of breath. For the shock and disgust, but it never comes. Instead he takes one in his mouth and sucks hard. Fuck, that feels amazing. I throw my head back in ecstasy. I've forgotten what it feels like.

I feel like I should be doing something, so I take the

hem of his t-shirt and pull it up, forcing him to stop what he's so fabulously doing, for me to yank it up over his head. Not so sexily, I must add.

I pull back to take in the view of his chest. His subtly bronzed, six pack of a chest. Fuck me, he must train hard. I have no idea how he finds the time between teaching, plays and tending to every need of Clara's. I trace my hands over his pecs, unable to comprehend that this absolute hunk wants little old me. It's crazy.

He takes my hand and leads me towards his bedroom while I'm still in a daze of disbelief. He pushes me gently back on the bed before stopping to take off his jeans and his boxers. His erect dick springs free. Holy mama! Well, if that isn't the most perfect dick I've ever seen.

I lift onto my elbows in an attempt to scoot further up the bed, but he stops me by pulling my thighs open. Then his mouth is on me. Holy fuck, this man has mad skills. No wonder Clara wanted the dude to marry her. No, no, stop thinking of her. *And how you've ruined her life.* I won't let her ruin this for me.

He licks me, slow and deliberate before sucking on my clit.

'My God, you're soaking,' he says proudly, looking up to give me a wink.

I can't help but blush. Then he's towering over me, kissing me again as he lines himself up and thrusts into me. With my arse on the edge of the bed and my legs clung

round him he's able to go deeper than anyone ever has.

I scream at every thrust, the feeling of fullness combined with the emotion of feeling cherished too much for my soul to bear. He rides me hard and relentlessly, his teeth gritting in the effort, but that doesn't stop him from caressing my cheek, pushing strands of hair from my face, kissing me gently. Small acts that show me this isn't just some dirty hook-up. This is real.

Before I know what's happening I'm coming, squeezing my legs so tight around his arse he actually grunts in pain. It's amazing and unbearable. Intense and too much. As he finds his last final thrusts and his own release I can't help but lie there, sated, and wonder what the hell have I got myself into?

Chapter 15

Monday 29th January

I still can't believe it. I slept with Hartley! I woke up next to his gorgeous face and then remembered that he was mine now. I know I should probably feel terrible for Clara, but for once I'm trying to just worry about myself. And the fact that if Hugh finds out, I'm not only fired, but I'll seriously piss off my best friend. Well, once she finds out what a risky mess Hugh has put them in.

I go to unlock the door to the pub when I find it open. That's weird. Have we been broken into? I look around for a potential weapon, but the only thing out here is some potted plants. I try to lift one up, but it must be the weight of a baby elephant. There's no way I'm getting that above my waist. Damn it.

The only thing I have in my bag is my phone. I take it

out and look back at the door. Should I call the police? But what if it's nothing and they tell me off for placing a prank call? No, I can't do that. I hate being told off.

Instead I dial 999 just in case I need to call them quickly and hold it above my head, reasoning with myself that I can use it as a weapon. Desperate times and all that.

I creep in, making sure every little footstep is placed on the floor delicately to make as little noise as possible. This old pub creaks when the bloody wind blows.

I walk slowly in to find the cleaner stood behind Clara. Holy fuck. She knows.

'Hiya, Nadine,' the cleaner says cheerily. 'I hope you don't mind, but I let in Miss Blumenkrantz for your appointment.'

'Oh... that's fine.' You just signed my death certificate, you silly cow.

Now that I look at her, she doesn't actually look how I imagined. If I'd just been dumped by my fiancé, I'd no doubt have big red-rimmed eyes and bags under them from crying my eyes out all night. But she looks... normal. Impassive. She's not even got the hard stare of someone about to kill somebody, which is what I can only assume she wants to do to me.

'Clara, hi.' I put my handbag down and twiddle with my rings to stop myself from having to look her in the eye. Actually, maybe I should have kept the handbag as a weapon. Crap, I knew I should have gone with Mia to those self-defence classes. But you never think you're going to be viciously attacked, do you? You also never think you're going to steal someone else's fiancé, but that ship has definitely sailed.

'Did you forget we had a meeting planned this morning to go through the flowers?' she asks, seemingly oblivious to what's happening to her.

Oblivious to the fact that I just spent the night with Hartley. There's no way on this earth she can know about us. In the midst of the passion last night I actually forgot to ask him what he said to her. Whether I was mentioned at all. I bloody hope not.

Maybe she's lulling me into a false sense of security before she pounces and rips my hair out. But either way she must know the wedding is cancelled. Right? She must be in shock. Complete and utter denial. Poor bitch.

'Um, no, I didn't forget. I just...' I can't make on like I know. Then she'll know I've spoken to Hartley. 'Yeah, I actually did forget. Sorry, few too many wines last night.' I fake a laugh. It sounds so unnatural and squeaky. I hate myself.

I go to my desk and start to shuffle a few papers, playing for time. How can she be acting like normal? She doesn't look like someone on the brink of a nervous breakdown. Her hair isn't bedraggled, instead its blow dried to perfection. He *did* break up with her, right? He didn't just tell me all of that yesterday, so I'd sleep with him?

Get one last shag in before saying I do. The idea has me feeling dizzy.

Should I say something? Try to find out if she does know and is just being crazy. Ah, I know.

I start clicking around on my computer. I flinch my head back slightly, like I've just seen something that shocks me.

'Oh, this is strange.'

She frowns, pouting her lips. 'What is it?'

I grimace. 'Uh, I've got an email here from Mr Valentine saying that the wedding has been cancelled.' I tilt my head to the side and purse my lips, an intense silence settling over us.

Her chin wobbles. Oh no, she's going to cry. I was not ready for this sort of emotion. Rage, yes. Upset, no. She bursts into tears, a bloody river flowing from her eyes.

As if I couldn't feel worse about myself. This whole thing was far easier when I could think of her as a using monster, but now seeing her as just another woman dumped. Well, it's got me feeling sick to my stomach.

'He's told me it's over,' she sobs, her mascara running under her eyes.

Looking at her like this, seeing the devastation I've caused first-hand is too much. I didn't think I could feel any worse, but I was wrong. My chest feels tight, my throat thick.

'I'm so sorry.' It's all I can offer. It doesn't even come

close to how remorseful I feel.

She droops her shoulders and sniffles. 'I just don't understand. It was all being sorted.' Her shoulders jump up and down as more tears fall. 'And we've told *everyone*. It's going to be so humiliating having to tell them it's cancelled.'

I cringe at the thought of it but can't help but feel better that her biggest concern is people finding out. A normal person would be heartbroken that the person they thought was their soulmate didn't love them anymore.

I swallow down the guilt, begging my quaking tongue to calm long enough for me to say something reassuring.

'The right people will stick by you,' I offer weakly.

'Not my bloody fiancé!' She throws her hand to her chest and rubs it as if having a heart attack. Probably just heartburn. 'He's off having some kind of quarter-life crisis!'

I really don't know what she wants me to say to her. I'm awful in situations like this, especially when it's my fault.

'If it helps at all I can give you your full deposit back?' I know it's a pathetic offer when her life is crumbling around her, but I feel like I want to offer her something. I should really have checked with Hugh first, but I'm sure Flo can talk him round if I get her a pretty cupcake.

She sniffs, staring down at her hands. 'It's not about the money. I just...' she looks up to the ceiling, her eyes glassy with yet more tears. 'I had this future all planned out

and now I feel as if it's been ripped out from underneath me.'

Yeah, and I'm the carpet ripper. I have to speak to Hartley. I can't be the cause of this woman's misery.

When I get home, I'm surprised to find Anna waiting outside my door. How the hell did she know where I lived?

'Anna?' I ask tentatively in case she's not here and the stress of the day has me hallucinating.

'Hi.' She smiles timidly, tucking her hair behind her ear.

'What are you doing here? How did you even know where I live?' Oops, I hope I didn't sound too unfriendly.

'Oh, I stalked you on Facebook. Yeah, you should really look into your privacy settings.'

'Are you serious?'

She rolls her eyes. 'Of course, I am.'

I walk past her to put the key in the door. 'Well, let me boil the kettle and you can help me with it.'

'Hiya, love,' Mum shouts from the kitchen. Ah, she's home. How the hell am I going to explain Anna?

I turn back to Anna who's still stood sheepishly on the doorstep. 'Well, come in then.'

She nods, swallows and follows me into the kitchen.

'I've got a brew on,' Mum says, turning to see us both. 'Oh, I didn't realise you were bringing a guest.'

I'm guessing she would have preferred Hartley, not a teenage girl.

'Yeah, Mum, this is Anna. She's from the school I've been helping at.'

Recognition registers on her face. 'I see. Nice to meet you, Anna.' She looks between the two of us. 'Are you girls still working on something for the play?'

'Err... no, actually,' Anna admits, scratching nervously at her neck. 'Nadine's been helping me with something else. Something a bit more... personal.'

'Ah,' Mum says with a grimace. 'Well in that case I'll leave you to make the tea for us and I'll go wait in the lounge.'

I smile back gratefully. 'Thanks, Mum.'

As soon as she's gone, Anna sits down at the table and smiles. 'Your mum seems really nice.'

'Oh, she is, bless her.' Sometimes I take for granted how lucky I am to have her and Dad. 'So anyway, what's up?'

'So, I told my parents,' she explains, biting her lip.

I flinch. 'How did they take it?'

She shakes her head comically from side to side. 'To say they took it badly is kind of an understatement.'

I raise my eyebrows. 'I'm gonna need a bit more than that.'

She sighs. 'They've told me I'm to have the baby adopted. Otherwise I'm on my own.'

'What do you mean, on your own?' She can't mean truly on her own, right?

'As in they'll kick me out,' she clarifies, her head dropping slowly onto the table.

I scoff. 'They can't be serious. That must be an empty threat, surely?'

To give their daughter an ultimatum like that when talking about something as serious as a child. It blows my mind how heartless some people can be.

She shakes her head. 'No, they're very serious. They even want me to go stay with my aunt and uncle in Italy until I've had the baby. Don't want the shame of everyone seeing.'

Jesus, what kind of parents are these? Some people don't deserve the title.

'But haven't you told them you want to keep it?'

Papa Don't Preach comes shooting into my head. I try to ignore it but find myself humming it ever so slightly anyway.

'They don't care. They've said I'm too young and the baby should be given to a responsible couple who desperately want a baby. And in a way, I can't disagree with them. If they kick me out I have nothing and no-one.'

I can't imagine feeling that desperate and alone. I may have been through shit, but I always knew that I had Florence and my family who would do anything to help me, regardless of the situation.

'Well actually...' We both look up to see Mum leaning into the room, having just said that. Has she been listening? 'You do have options.' She sits down at the table with us.

Anna raises her eyebrows at me.

'So, you've been listening then, Mother?' I laugh, unable to hide me being pissed at the intrusion of privacy. I'm trying to get Anna to trust me. 'And what would your magic solution be?'

She shrugs. 'Move in here. We can help out.'

My mouth drops open. 'Mum, are you serious? I don't think you should be offering things to Anna that you're not one hundred percent sure about.'

What the hell is she doing offering this to her without even talking to me first?

'I'm sure,' she nods confidently. 'How could I live with myself knowing this girl wants her baby but is being forced to give it away?'

'I don't even know you,' Anna says warily. 'But you'd just take me in?'

She nods, a kind smile on her lips. 'Every child is a blessing, Anna. We have a spare bedroom and I can tell just by Nadine's face that she's taken with you. Let us help you.'

She bursts into tears. 'How can you be so nice when my own parents treat me like a stupid child?'

I rub her back. 'Because my mum is pretty amazing. I think they broke the mould when they made her.' She smiles back at me, wiping at her tear-stained face. 'Why don't we arrange to see your parents and have a chat with them? I'm still not completely convinced that they'll kick you out.'

'And if they do?' she asks, fear settling in her eyes.

I look to Mum. She nods confidently. 'Then we pack a bag and get you out of there.'

I just hope to God Dad's on board with the random pregnant teenager potentially moving in.

Chapter 16

Tuesday 30th January

I don't want to go into work today. I can't face any happy couples when I know I've helped split one up. Maybe I shouldn't be allowed near them with my groom stealing abilities.

I'd quite happily wallow in bed and my own self-pity for the day, but not only do I have work, but my younger sister Lydia is coming around today, fresh from her honeymoon.

A normal sister would be excited about a sibling's news from their honeymoon, but not me. Don't get me wrong, I don't have any bad feelings towards her. I actually feel sorry for her after her disastrous wedding. It just burns a little that she's three years younger than me and already has her happily ever after. Especially when I'm so intent on ruining

others.

My one chance at love and it comes hand in hand with crushing guilt at having sacrificed someone else's happiness for my own.

I force myself out of bed and shower quickly, hearing the front door go while I'm drying my hair. I throw a pair of flannel pyjamas on, wanting to at least be cosy, and head downstairs, plastering on my fake smile.

Lydia's at the kitchen table with Mum, already having a cuppa.

'Hey, Nads,' she says jumping up to hug me. 'I'm so glad you're finally here.'

Jeez, God forbid I take a shower. I force myself not to sigh out loud.

'I have some exciting news,' she beams, sitting down to look between me and Mum.

She must have got her wedding photos back. From her excitement I'm guessing they managed to take some where she doesn't look stoned. I've become more jaded from dealing with her wedding than I have from a whole year of dealing with demanding brides at work.

'I'm expecting!' she gushes, jumping up to standing again, to jump on the spot.

My mouth drops open. 'Expecting... some more photos back from the photographer or...?' I don't want to offer the alternative.

I can't think of the alternative.

Mum's eyebrows are quirked in anticipation, glancing to me every half a second to sense my reaction.

'Expecting, as in I'm pregnant!' she says in triumph, her grin so large I'm scared it's going to split her face in two.

My stomach feels like I just swallowed a brick. She's pregnant? My baby sister is having a baby.

'Wow,' Mum says, seemingly as taken aback as me. 'Congratulations, love.' She stands up and brings her into a slow hug, eyeing me as she does.

I hate that look. The drooped eyelids, the concern on her pursed lips. The look of sympathy. From my own mother.

But my mum is the only one who understands. I am, after all, her baby and when I hurt, she hurts. I know that better than anyone.

Taking a deep breath, I give myself a rapid pep talk. This is good news. This is your baby sister sharing her happiness with you. I need to embrace it.

She takes herself out of Mum's embrace and comes for me, not a hint of concern in her beaming smile. She's never been good at thinking about others. I hug her back with as much enthusiasm as I can muster, but it's as if my whole body has gone numb in its own effort of protecting itself.

'And it's twins.'

My body goes rigid. She's having fucking *twins?* What, one baby isn't enough for Lydia? Jesus fucking Christ.

I pull back, showing my teeth in what I hope looks like a smile and not a grimace. 'Amazing news! Congrats.'

She frowns briefly. 'And you're definitely happy for me? You know, after...'

'Belle,' I say out loud. 'You can say her name. After Belle.'

She nods, her eyes sympathetic.

'Of course, I'm happy for you,' I say sincerely, because I am really. The fact that I'm also devastated and extremely jealous won't be mentioned.

She starts getting scan pictures out and talking to Mum about how it was so unexpected, but how they're over the moon. Jesus, she wasn't even trying to get pregnant.

The room feels like it's closing in on me, my lungs tight as if the oxygen is being sucked out of them. I have to get out of here. I can't do this right now.

I start backing away. 'I'm so sorry. I just remembered I need to do something right now.'

'Really?' she asks, clearly crushed that I don't want to see my nieces or nephews.

'Yeah, I'm so sorry, but I said I'd...' Quickly Nadine, think of something. 'Feed Kelly's cats this weekend.'

Really Nadine? That's all your brain can come up with? Feeding some bloody cats!

'Surely that's not an emergency?' she asks with an outraged snort.

Of course, she's right.

'Oh, but it is,' I stutter, walking backwards out of the room. 'I haven't fed them since Friday. I just hope I don't find them starved to death.'

Grabbing my coat, keys, and bag, I leave before I burst into tears in front of them. It's only as I'm walking to the car that I realise I'm still in my flannel pyjamas. I consider turning back, but I'd only have to answer more questions that I can't face right now.

I get in the car and start driving, unsure of my destination. My first thought is to go around Flo's, but what if Hugh is there? She has a husband now. I can't just drop around. I don't want to breakdown in front of him. I know Kelly and Mia will be at work. That leaves... oh, that's right, no-one.

Instead I find myself parking outside a Tesco extra in a part of town I'm not familiar with. I've no concept of how long I've been driving or where I am. My body's just been on autopilot.

I lean my head against the steering wheel and force myself to take a deep breath.

This is fine. Nothing is happening that you didn't expect after Lydia getting married. I mean, sure, it's a hell of a lot faster than I was anticipating, and I didn't expect twins—but I still shouldn't feel this shaken to my core.

It just seems that everywhere I look there are pregnant women in my life. Babies that are going to be born that I'll have to watch grow up. Grow up and get to do everything that my Belle never had a chance to do.

Chocolate. I need chocolate. I do my coat up as best I can and decide to brave Tesco. With me not knowing exactly where I am hopefully I won't see anyone I know.

I walk in quickly heading straight towards the chocolate aisle. I grab the largest packet of Dairy Milk and head for the till. There's a queue so I have to pause and deal with the funny looks from judgy customers.

Yeah, yeah, I'm in my pyjamas. Get over it.

'Nadine?'

I freeze, scared to turn around and find who it is that knows me.

I slowly pivot round until I'm face to face with Hartley. Just seeing his gorgeous face creased in concern makes me crumble. I break down in tears, the weight of everything heavy on my shoulders. Breaking up a relationship, putting my career in danger, and now finding out my own sister is going to have not one, but two babies. My life is a disaster, and I know it.

He pulls me into his chest, wrapping his arms around me tightly. 'Oh babe, what's happened?'

I sob, my shoulders shaking a ridiculous amount. 'I'm fine,' I insist weakly.

He scoffs, his chest rumbling beneath me. 'Yeah, you look fine.'

He takes my Dairy Milk from me, puts down a fiver at the till and then walks me out of the shop.

'You're coming back to mine,' he insists, guiding me towards his car.

I try to protest, but I know he won't have it and I don't have the energy to fight anyone right now. It's easier to just go along with it.

I sit in the car in silence, looking out the window at the grey and dreary day. What a mess I've made of my life.

I know before he even pulls up that I have to end things with him. I have to let him go, let him marry Clara, who he was destined to marry all along. Before I fell into his life and fucked everything up. I'm just a bitter woman who deep down only wants to make people as miserable as me.

He puts the key into the door and leads me, hand on my back, into his flat.

'I can't do this, Hartley,' I blurt out to him as soon as I'm inside.

He frowns. 'Huh?'

I walk into the sitting room, not bothering to take my coat off. 'Clara came into work yesterday crying her eyes out. I can't do it. I can't be responsible for ruining a relationship.'

He takes my shaking hands. 'Nadine, I keep telling you, the relationship wasn't going anywhere for a while.'

'So you keep telling me,' I snap. 'But be honest, can you say hand on heart, that if you hadn't met me you would have still broken up with her?'

He looks at the floor. It's enough to tell me he'd have

carried on with it. Or at least considered it if I'd not come along.

'That's enough of an answer for me.' I turn and head for the door.

He grabs my hand and pulls me back into him. 'Stop! I can't lose you.' His eyes are desperate, pleading with me more than his words ever can.

I force myself to break away from them. 'I'm sorry, Hartley, but don't you see? Me and you were never meant to be. You were never mine to lose. It's wrong.'

He cups my face with his hands, staring into my soul. 'How can something that feels so right be wrong?'

I gulp, my eyes stinging from all the tears. 'Because you're a cheater.'

'Am I?' he asks, his forehead pinched. 'I broke up with her before sleeping with you. Doesn't that count for something?'

I shake my head, my chest aching. 'It doesn't matter. Once the story gets out, it'll be that we were having a fully-fledged affair. It will ruin my whole career. Hugh will fire me and no-one's going to want to employ the wedding planner that stole the groom.'

He starts manically pacing, wringing his hands. 'No-one will care. Who cares about a career?' He stops to take my hands, his eyes pleading with me. 'Surely happiness is more important?'

I push him away using all my energy and cross my

arms, turning away from him to wipe my weepy nose. If I keep looking into his eyes, I know he'll hypnotise me into staying and I'll be naked again in less than twenty minutes. I have to push him away instead.

'So, you're just dismissing my career like it's nothing? What if it was you being fired?'

He frowns. 'Why would I be fired?'

I have to make him see what it would be like for the situation to be reversed. 'What if I was one of your students? Then you'd be fired for sure.'

'Then it would be totally inappropriate,' he snaps, like I'm insane, arms crossed over his chest. 'Of course, it would.'

'And this isn't?' He stares back at me, his eyes begging me to come back to him. 'I'm sorry, Hartley, but I've dropped everything for a man before and look how that worked out.'

He pinches his lips together. 'I wouldn't know, because you don't share anything with me. You're a closed book, Nadine. Why won't you open up to me?'

My chest aches from everything I haven't told him. Everything I should and never will.

'Some wounds are better left alone.'

I turn and run.

Chapter 17

I wake up to twenty-two missed calls from him. Bless him, you can't say he's not bothered. He just needs to realise that this is for the best. That it's going to hurt at first, but in the long run he'll thank me. Not that it makes me feel much better. Who knew that my already broken heart could be shattered into mere smithereens?

When I get to work, I find Clara sat outside on the bench. Not this again! When is she going to realise that it's over? Well, unless he's already changed his mind, cut his losses and agreed to marry her again. Wow, that idea hurts more than I thought it would.

She spots me as I walk over, her eyes protruding out of their sockets. 'You bitch!' she screams jumping to her feet.

I look behind me, wondering if she was shouting at

someone else.

But it's me she's looking at, while she shakes with rage. 'You little fucking whore! What kind of wedding planner steals the groom, huh?!'

The world starts spinning around me. She knows. How the hell can she know?

'Err… what are you talking about?' I ask, attempting to play dumb. It's not hard. I have no idea how she could have known. Did someone see us kissing after the float crash? Grass us up?

'I'm talking about you, home-wrecker.' She stands right in front of me, jabbing a pointy, perfectly manicured finger into my chest. 'Getting into my fiancé's bed, and his mind, for that matter. Convincing him that he shouldn't marry me.'

'I didn't! I swear!' I back away, noting how she's baring her teeth like a dog. I wouldn't put it past her to physically attack me. Not that I don't deserve it.

She leans on one leg, her hand resting on her hip. 'So, you're trying to tell me you never hooked-up?' She lowers her head to study my reaction.

'Err…' I look from side to side, my eyes rapidly blinking of their own accord. 'Look, whatever happened between us happened after he'd finished with you.'

Like that sounds any better. I hate myself.

'What?' she snarls, laughing cruelly, an edge to it that spreads goosepimples over my arms. 'You mean Sunday?

Mere hours after he'd decided to dump me? Pretty fucking coincidental isn't it?'

She's got me there.

'I... I...' my words stammer out, my throat choosing this moment to close in on itself. 'I didn't mean for this to happen.'

'You bitch!'

Before I can register what's happening, she's launched herself at me like some kind of manic spider monkey. I fall to the floor as she attempts to pull my hair out from the roots.

'Aaarrgh!' I scream, the sting unbearable. 'Leave me alone, you crazy bitch!'

She slaps me round the face manically. I hold my hands up over my face, attempting to shield myself. The worst thing is that I feel I should just take it, lower my hands and let her beat me. I know I deserve it.

'Get off her,' someone yells. I still daren't move my hands in case she takes the opportunity to gouge an eye out.

When she's finally off me, I quickly scramble to my feet. Hugh is holding her back, his face tense from trying to restrain her.

'What the hell is going on here?' he demands, looking between the both of us.

'She...' Clara roars, pointing at me, her eyes ablaze. 'stole my fucking fiancé!'

Hugh almost laughs as if the very idea is ridiculous.

'I'm sure that's not right.' He looks to me, rolling his eyes. Then he stills, taking in what I'm guessing must be my guilty expression. 'Right, Nadine?'

'Um...' I look down at the floor with a wince. Why do I find it so hard to lie to people's faces? It's really not a good quality for a groom stealing bitch. I'll have to work on that.

'What?' He releases her, the shock consuming him. She attempts to lunge for me again. He thankfully catches her just in time. 'Calm down, Clara, or I'll have to call the police.'

She takes a deep breath as if to try to calm herself. 'Fine. You know what? Fuck you. You're not even worth it. Hartley will come back when he's sick of your whorish pussy. You know what they say, sometimes they have steak at home, but they still fancy a quick burger.'

Did she just call me a burger? I've never been so offended on behalf of my vagina in my life.

'You better persuade him to find his lost mind again,' she continues, her face getting red and blotchy. 'I will be marrying him. Unless you want the whole of London to hear about the groom stealing whore of a wedding planner, I suggest you start working on it!'

She flounces off towards her car while I sigh in relief, pleased for the release of the immediate danger.

Hugh looks at me, his mouth slack, his eyes wide. 'Tell me this is bullshit. Tell me it's not true?'

I look down at my sweaty palms. 'It's... well... it's

complicated.'

He wrinkles his nose up. 'Complicated? What the fuck, Nads? You've stolen her bloke?'

'No!' I cry. 'I didn't steal anyone. It just...' I put my hands over my eyes, attempting to block this nightmare out. 'It just kind of happened and not before they'd broken up.'

He closes his eyes and drops his head forward. 'But you were involved in the breakup?'

The look of disappointment on his face is too much to bear. I look away, my eyes misting up.

'For fuck's sake, Nadine. What were you thinking?' he asks, his voice low and disgruntled. 'This could ruin the business we've just spent the last year building up. Did you even think of that?' He pinches the bridge of his nose, closing his eyes as if in pain.

'Of course, I thought of that!' He has no idea how long I've agonised over this.

His eyes open to reveal a new stony expression in them. 'But you thought fuck it anyway?' He sighs. 'Jesus, Nadine, this is so unlike you.'

'Exactly!' I scream back. 'Don't you think this is a big deal to me too? Don't you think I've agonised over this? Trust me when I say I haven't taken this lightly.'

'I don't care, Nadine,' he snaps. 'Either break up with him or forget about your job.'

My mouth drops to the floor. He's willing to fire me? I don't care that I've already broken it off, barely before it's begun. Does he really value me so little he'd get rid of me that rashly? After me dedicating a whole year of my life to building this business up with him?

My phone rings again, Hartley's name flashing up. I turn away from Hugh and answer it, a new fury taking over my body. I'm about to tear him a new arsehole for not warning me.

'Hartley! How could you have done this to me?' I cry down the phone, my eyes clouded with unshed tears. Now I think of it, did he do it to deliberately hurt me? Some kind of payback for me breaking it off?

'Oh God,' he sighs down the phone. 'She got to you, huh?'

'Yes!' I shout, my voice breaking into a small sob. 'Why the fuck didn't you warn me?'

'That's what I've been trying to do, if you would have just answered your fucking phone.'

Oh no. This is my own fault. What kind of sane woman ignores twenty-two missed calls? There I was thinking he was just trying to win me back, but he was trying to warn me that his psycho ex was on the way.

I walk out of the pub and sit down on the bench, tears pricking at my eyes. 'Everything's ruined. She's going to badmouth me all around town. Hugh's pissed with me.' I turn to see he's let himself into the pub. Probably already trying to do some damage control. 'This was all a mistake. Just one big mistake.'

'I'm so sorry, Nadine.' I hear the anguish in his voice.

'Yeah,' I sniffle. 'So am I.'

I came straight home after speaking to Hartley. Hugh had basically fired me, and I couldn't face him. I went home, telling Mum I was just feeling overwhelmed, and that Hugh had given me the rest of the week off to de-stress. She was suspicious as hell, asking why I was feeling overwhelmed but backed down when I nearly bit her head off. I hate that I've taken it out on her of all people.

My mood is put on hold though when Anna calls asking if we fancy going round to speak to her parents. It's obviously weighing heavily on her mind so me and Mum quickly get ready and head to her smart semi-detached house. Before we even get a chance to ring the doorbell, she's answering the door.

'Hi,' she whispers, biting her lip. 'Are you sure you guys want to do this?'

'Of course,' I smile, faking confidence. In reality I'm shitting it. They could go mental and punch me in the face. I'd like to see them go for my mum, I'd turn ninja on their arse. No one touches my mama! 'Do they know we're coming?'

She shakes her head, her face deathly pale. 'No. I've been too nervous to tell them.'

'Okay. Here goes nothing then.'

We follow her into the back where we find her parents in an open plan kitchen that must have cost a fortune, all granite worktops and sleek glossed cabinets. It definitely pisses all over our small kitchen at home with its broken cupboard doors that have needed fixing for a long time.

Anna clears her throat. 'Mum, Dad, this is Nadine, and her mum, Debra.'

Her mum's the first to react, pushing her jet-black hair behind her ears, her eyes narrowed in suspicion. 'Oh. Hello.'

'They're here to talk about the baby,' Anna says, so pale I'm expecting her to pass out at any minute. I hope she's drinking enough water.

Her dad lowers his head to stare at us. Her mum on the other hand seems to realise quickly what we're here for, but she looks happy. What's going on?

'Oh, I see what's happening here,' she says, a wide grin on her face. 'Anna, you've found someone to adopt the baby!' She jumps up from the stool and comes over to shake our hands, nearly pulling my arm from the socket.

'Oh, um... that's not actually what we're here for,' I try to explain.

'Oh.' She frowns. 'Okay, but then...' she looks back at her husband, 'I don't really understand why you're here.'

Mum stands forward. 'We're here to discuss your options for Anna.'

Her Mum scoffs. 'She doesn't have any options. She's

knocked up at sixteen.'

Mum smiles sadly. 'Would you honestly happily just hand over your grandchild without a second thought?' I can tell from her tone that she's disgusted.

'Oh, I've thought about it intensely,' her mum retorts. 'How my sixteen-year-old daughter has no idea how to raise a baby. How a happy couple, desperate for a baby would raise it with all the love, money and attention it deserves.'

I have to talk up here. 'But how do you think your grandchild will react when it grows up and tracks you both down? Hears you forced Anna to give them up. How do you think that child is going to feel?'

'Grateful that I gave it a chance in life!' she snaps.

'It's Anna's body,' I insist. 'And if she wants to keep the baby, I really think you should consider supporting her. There's nothing you can't get through.'

She scoffs, looking at me like I'm an idiot. 'Save me the rubbish. This is not in her plans. The decision has been made.'

'Only because you've given her no other option,' I argue. She wasn't lying when she said she's really up against it with parents this stubborn.

Mum stands closer to her, offering a calming hand on her shoulder. 'I myself have lost a grandchild.' My stomach drops. Anna doesn't know about this and I wish she didn't have to. 'And let me tell you it's the worst feeling in the world.'

She smiles back at her with an eye roll. 'I'm so sorry that happened to you, but it doesn't change my mind.'

Mum sighs, clearly admitting defeat. We're not going to change their minds.

'Well then, Anna has been given another option by us. She can move in with us and we'll support her.'

Her dad's face goes bright red, a vein in his forehead throbbing. 'I don't bloody think so. She's our daughter and our problem.'

'I'm not a problem, Dad!' Anna shouts, suddenly finding her voice. 'I want to keep this baby and if you won't let me, then I'll go with this family. This family I hardly know who seem to care more about me than you do.'

'Don't be ridiculous,' he growls. 'We only want what's best for you. What kind of job are you going to get with no qualifications?'

She sighs. 'I've got the rest of my life to get qualifications. I'm keeping my baby.'

There goes *Papa Don't Preach* lyrics in my head again.

'I'm packing a bag and I'm going.' She hesitates a second, her eyes glassy with unshed tears. 'This is your last chance to have me in your life.'

Her dad remains strong, barely flinching. I can tell her mum is slightly more anxious behind him, but she doesn't speak up. Instead they watch as Anna collects her things and we take her back to ours.

I really can't believe they'd just let her leave like that.

Some people don't deserve to be parents.

When we're in the car, I lean back to Anna. 'Are you okay?'

'Yeah,' she nods, a single tear escaping down her cheek. 'I just...' she sighs. 'I kind of was holding onto a small hope that they'd fight for me.'

'I know, hun. I know.'

Chapter 18

Wednesday 31st January

I feel so bad for Anna. She put on a brave face last night but when she went to bed in her new bedroom, I heard her crying. I think I'll take her shopping later. Buy her a few bits to make it feel more like her space. God knows the daisy patterned bedspread we've had for years isn't the most glam in the world. Especially for a teenager with her life falling apart around her.

All the drama with Anna did put everything into perspective for me though. I've decided that I've let my stupid emotions take over and delete out any rational thoughts. I have to speak to Hartley, tell him once and for all that we will never be together. I could still hear the hope in his voice yesterday. He's clearly hanging onto some idea that we can still work.

I have no idea how I'll do that, but I know I'm going to have to break his heart. For real this time. It's for the best. He was content enough before I came along, confusing his fickle male brain.

I need to concentrate on myself and looking after Anna. In a weird way I'm glad for the new project. How awful is that? I'm leaning on this sixteen-year-old girl more than she is on me.

I'm waiting outside his flat before he leaves for work. Okay, I might have been awake since five worrying. But it's better to just get it over and done with, right?

'Nadine?' he checks, his face lighting up when he sees me, looking all kinds of delicious in a dark-grey suit and pale-blue shirt with an open neck. If I peered just right, I'd be able to see the start of his chest.

As if noticing I'm checking him out, he grabs my face with his hands and plants a quick kiss on my lips before crushing me against his chest in a hug. 'I'm so glad you came to me. We can talk this all out.'

I feel myself well up at the idea of breaking his heart when he's still so hopeful. The warmth of his hard body against me is enough to make me feel I belong here. But I don't. That doesn't stop me wanting to savour this. Savour him one last time.

I kiss him slowly and deeply, savouring the taste of him. I shut my eyes and drink him in, memorising the feel of his plump lips on mine. His hands are wrapped around my face, cherishing me.

The resistance drains from me, drop by drop. Just one more time. Just one more time to say goodbye.

He keeps me in his arms while scrambling to unlock the door. He pushes me in backwards, the warmth of his body melting my last shred of resistance. His hands delve into my hair, grasping and pulling urgently. He yanks my head back to gain access to my neck. He peppers kisses down it while I moan like a wanton whore.

He kicks the door shut, his hands finding my hips and lifting me off the floor. I automatically wrap my legs around his waist and immerse myself in the warmth of his neck, his fresh masculine scent causing me to lick him.

He crushes me against the wall, finding the buttons of my blouse and instead choosing to rip it apart. Just seeing his strength turns me on even more. I'm gonna be wetter than an otter's pocket in a minute.

He shoves my skirt up my body while I fumble with his trousers, yanking them and his boxers down. Then he's lining himself up and thrusting into me. No preamble or warning.

He fucks me hard, so hard my head is repeatedly smashed against the wall. I half wonder if I'll have a head wound by the end of it, but it feels too good right now to care.

His legs must be killing him because soon he's grabbing me and moving us to the back of his sofa. He plants my butt on the back of it and continues to hammer into me. It's hard and fast. Animalistic even. We're both just working on autopilot, letting our bodies take over.

Chills starts at the base of my spine, my hair standing on end, and spread all the way up to my head until my mouth is gaping open and I'm panting like a rabid dog. My head starts spinning, my body shaking uncontrollably. It's almost painful. I eventually fall off the teetering cliff and shatter around him.

A serene sense of calm takes over me. I crush myself into his chest as he finally finds his release. I could stay here forever, happily safe in his arms, but I know that's not our reality.

It's now or never. Never would be preferred, but this is what's best for everyone. I push him away gently, pushing my skirt back down and readjusting my blouse. Time to be a hard bitch.

'We can't do this again,' I say staring at the wall.

There's an awkward pause. 'What are you talking about?'

I turn to see his features downcast, his eyes heavy in confusion. Damn it, why did I have to turn to him? I should have just said it and ran.

I swallow hard, my mouth dry. 'Sorry, Hartley, but I can't do this.'

His face has turned ashen. Maybe I should have left it a bit longer after the sex.

'Yes, you can,' he insists. 'Me and you together, we can do anything as long as we've got each other.'

'No,' I say sternly. 'We're not together. I'm sorry, but this was just sex.'

He laughs, his eyes not convinced. 'Come on, you know this was more than that.'

I shake my head, standing my ground, even though I want nothing more than to run into his arms and let him love me.

'Maybe to you, but not to me. I'm sorry, but I got caught up in being wanted again. I used you to get over my ex and now that I have I see that it's him I want.'

Just uttering this lie has me feeling sick to my stomach.

He looks like his world has collapsed around him. His chin wobbles, his eyes distant.

'Look,' I continue, 'we both used each other to get over something, but I honestly think you should just go back to Clara. Apologise. She'll take you back.'

'Don't you see that I don't want fucking Clara!' he explodes, throwing his arms in the air. 'What do I have to do to get it through your thick skull?'

'That's no bother to me either way,' I snap harshly, not recognising the coldness in my own voice. 'I won't be here.'

I stand up, grab my bag and bolt for the door, the first happiness of the last two years left behind in that room.

Chapter 19

Saturday 3rd Feb

Clara took immense pleasure in re-booking an appointment with me at the pub.

Hugh says he's forgiven me and given me my job back, but I know he's still pissed. Florence managed to talk him down to a certain extent and I think the fact that the wedding is still going ahead stands somewhat in my favour.

But it's made me realise I can't stay working here long term. I've seen what I'm worth to him now; not much. I can't stay working for someone like that, regardless of who he's married to.

I made sure Flo and Hugh were at my first appointment with Clara, so she couldn't openly attack me. She smugly told me that the wedding was back on and to carry on with the previous arrangements.

I can't lie and say it didn't gut me that he went back to her. Of course, I told him to, but a large part of me hoped he was so in love with me that he couldn't even entertain the idea of seeing her again, let alone marrying her.

So, the last few days I've been hiding my heartache and splitting my time working my arse off to make sure it's the best wedding I can make it and helping Anna settle in at home.

I owe Clara that much. I've done every gory design detail Clara's requested and against my better judgement, I have to admit that it looks amazing. Even the life-size ice sculptures look beautiful and not tacky.

It's all set up and I'm just sneaking out the door when Flo grabs me. 'Where the hell are you going?'

'I'm leaving,' I say, stating the obvious. 'Jill's in charge. I can't stay and witness him marrying her.'

Her eyes soften. 'Don't you think he deserves to see you one last time? To be given his full options?'

I scoff. She's ridiculous. 'Flo, you know I'm not one of his options. I can't be.'

'You can!' she shouts, taking my hand tenderly. 'For God's sake, Nadine. You're always doing what's best for everyone else. Don't listen to Hugh. Don't fuck this up over the fear of a job. Something that could replace you within a week.'

I snort. 'Gee, thanks.'

She raises her eyebrows. 'This could be your happy

ending. Your one true love. Don't let any loyalty towards me or Hugh stop you.'

I scoff. 'Flo, you watch far too many Disney movies.'

She snorts a laugh. 'Yeah, well I'm glad I do. Look at how it worked out for me and Hugh.'

She's so far out of reality it's unreal.

'We're not all you and Hugh. Some of us aren't so lucky.'

'But you could be,' she insists, pleading with her eyes. 'Just stay and talk to him before he goes to that altar.'

I think about it for a moment. I suppose I could give myself this. It's not like I'm planning on objecting to the ceremony. I could just be there and see his reaction. He's sure to shoot me down with how we left things anyway.

'But how can I do that to Clara? She deserves better than the woman that tried to steal her man attending her wedding.'

'She deserves nothing!' she shrieks in outrage. 'Do you know that woman told me I looked bloated the other day? What kind of dickhead tells a pregnant woman they look bloated?'

I smile. God, I love her. I pull her into a hug, appreciating for a moment every little thing about my bestie.

'Okay. I'll go wait with the registrar. Call me when he arrives.'

♡♥♡

He's twenty minutes late for his own wedding. Everyone knows I hate tardiness. This is taking the piss though. Flo is sitting with the guests, shrugging in confusion. Could he really not turn up?

The back doors of the barn suddenly fling open. All of us turn, expecting to see Hartley, but instead we're met with a furious looking Clara. She looks stunning in a huge princess gown, so big she has to turn sideways to get in the door.

'Where is she?' she screams.

Uh-oh, she can't be looking for me. Can she? 'Where is that little whore?'

Oops. She's definitely looking for me.

Our eyes meet across the room, her face turning thunderous. 'What the hell did you say to him? Huh? What on earth did you do?'

'I... I...'

Everyone in the room is staring at me.

Florence suddenly throws up, splashing the guests sat next to her. They rush to get out of her way.

'Jesus, Flo, are you okay?' I ask across the room, trying to get to her.

'Don't look at her, whore!' Clara shouts, barrelling down the aisle, almost in my face already. 'Look at me. Tell me what you did with your magic vagina to stop my fiancé from marrying me!'

Everyone in the crowd gasps. Well, this is humiliating.

Florence stands up to come over towards me but stops to throw up on another guest. Jesus, woman! It's like she's possessed!

'I've done nothing. I haven't spoken to Hartley since I broke it off with him.'

Everyone in the crowd starts whispering amongst themselves. Clara had obviously held back this bit of information.

The doors suddenly burst open again. The whole crowd turns, expecting Hartley. Instead there's some other guy in a suit. Who the hell is this and why is he making such a dramatic entrance?

'Stop the wedding!' he shouts theatrically, waving his hands in the air.

The guests gasp again. Jesus, this really is turning into a shit show. We should have been recording this.

'Edward?' Clara gasps. 'What the hell are you doing here?'

'Don't marry him,' he pleads, running towards her. 'You know it's really me that you love.'

She glances around at everyone, her cheeks pink. 'Shut up, Edward!' she hisses.

'No, I won't shut up anymore,' he declares strongly, taking her hand. 'I love you and I know that you love me too.'

'It was just sex!' she screams, loud enough for everyone to hear.

Everyone takes a collective gasp.

Her father stands up, a vein in his neck protruding. 'Edward. You mean to tell me you've been having an affair with my daughter?'

Oh my God. He must work with them. The plot thickens.

'I have, Sir,' he nods, squaring his shoulders. 'And I love her more than life itself.'

Her dad sits down, his eyes closed. 'Jesus, I need a drink.'

'For fuck's sake, Edward,' Clara snaps, before turning on her heel and flouncing out. He follows on behind her like a little lap puppy.

Florence is suddenly at my side, still looking green. 'So, Hartley never even turned up. Doesn't that tell you something?' she says with a knowing smile.

She's right. And there I have been feeling bad about Clara and the whole time she's been sleeping with Edward! That two-faced little bitch. Not that I can talk.

'I agree,' Hugh says, suddenly behind me.

I stare at him aghast. What the hell is happening here? He's been warning me to stay away from the beginning.

'Nadine, I have a big apology to make.' He looks towards the doors that Clara just flounced out of. 'I can't believe I've been such an arse to you when Clara was fucking that guy all along.'

'And...' Florence says encouragingly.

He swallows. 'And I was wrong to judge you in the first place. I know you well enough to know that you're always putting other people first. The one time you think about your own happiness and I treat you appallingly. Forgive me?'

I smile weakly back at him. He has far more grovelling to do before I can ever start to trust him again, but for the sake of Florence I nod.

'I have to see him,' I admit to her.

She smiles. 'You go, girl.' And then she vomits on my shoes.

Chapter 20

I go straight round his even though my shoes are still yucky with vomit. I only managed to rinse them with water. They really need to go in the bin, but they'll do for now.

Mia's promised to look after Florence and take her home. I need to see Hartley and find out what the hell he's playing at standing up Clara on their wedding day. Even I didn't think he was that heartless.

Leaving my shoes in the car, I walk up the stairs to his apartment barefoot. I'm aware I'll look crazy, but hell, I'm past that now.

I knock on the door, my stomach sick with fear. He might not even be here. He could be halfway round the world by now, but something tells me he'd stick around. Hartley wouldn't just leave his students like that.

He answers the door, his hair wayward and down. His

eyes widen when he spots me.

'Nadine?' he croaks, his voice is as if he hasn't spoken for days. 'What are you doing here?'

I lean on one hip. 'What are *you* doing here, more like? You're supposed to be getting married.'

He frowns. 'You know full well I split up with Clara weeks ago. What the hell are you talking about?'

What the hell is going on here?

'Yeah, but... you got back together,' I explain with a nod. 'You were supposed to show up today.' Wait, now I'm more confused. He keeps looking back at me with a grimace.

'Nadine, I literally have no idea what you're talking about. I think you should come in.' He holds the door open. Is this a trick? What the hell is happening here?

I walk in and sit on the edge of the sofa.

'Why do you have no shoes?' he asks with raised eyebrows, the hint of a smirk on his lips.

'I think I'll be the one to ask the questions, here, bucko.'

Bucko? *Who am I?*

'Okay.' He stands, his arms folded over his chest. 'Go ahead.'

I take a deep breath. 'Did you get back together with Clara?'

'No.' He didn't look to the left or the right when answering. I forget which side it is that tells you if they're lying, but in this case, he kept eye contact. That must mean the truth, right?

'Not, ever?'

'Never.' He shakes his head. 'She's persisted in trying. Even told me to turn up today and marry her, but she's crazy. I've told her I don't love her and that I wouldn't be doing it. If she's nuts enough to carry on with the wedding, that's nothing to do with me.'

Wow, so he really didn't run back to her. Could it be that he does still love me?

'But, I thought...?'

'You thought, what?' he asks, his eyes drooped. 'That I'd just go running back to her after you told me it was over? Nadine, how many times do I have to tell you? You weren't just some distraction from getting married. You're the real thing, the queen of my heart. I love you, and I don't care if it takes you years to realise it. Whenever you do, I'll be waiting. I'd rather have no-one than someone I'm not completely crazy about.'

Wow. That guy can give a speech.

'You... you love me?' I can't help but gasp.

'Of course, I do.' He sits down next to me. 'Why do you have so much trouble believing that?'

I think back to Joshua. He said he loved me but then was quick to leave me in my moment of need.

He deserves to know the whole story. Then we'll see if he really wants to stick around.

I take a deep breath. 'Look, you have to understand that I come with a lot of baggage. Like a lot.'

He grabs hold of my hands. They feel amazing in his large warm ones. 'I'll take it all. Just tell me. Are you...' he swallows hard, 'back with your ex?'

I scoff. 'No! of course not.'

'But you said...'

'I only said that so you'd go back to Clara and marry her. I couldn't live knowing I'd broken up your relationship.'

'That's one of the reasons I love you. Always thinking about everyone else, but never yourself. But, I need to know, are you really over your ex?'

'This is where it gets complicated.'

He squeezes my hand. 'I'm listening.'

I take a deep breath and force myself to tell him the one thing that gives him the power to break me. I know now that if I bare my soul to him and he rejects me it's going to hurt like nothing else.

'Me and Joshua were together five years when I fell pregnant.'

His eyes widen to twice the size, but he quickly attempts to recover.

I carry on, wanting to get it out before I chicken out. 'Even though it wasn't planned we were over the moon. We'd never been happier. But that all changed when Belle was born.'

'What happened?'

A tear slips down my cheek. 'She... she was born a sleeping angel. She died while still inside me.'

His face drops, his mouth ajar. 'Oh my God.'

I crush my eyes shut, attempting to block out the pain. The memory of it that feels like just yesterday.

'I can't even begin to describe to you how devastated we were.' He nods, rubbing my hand with his thumb in reassuring circles. I look down at our hands, unable to look him in the eye anymore. 'He blamed me.'

'Huh?'

I nod, still not wanting to look into what I know will be his heartbroken eyes.

'He did. He never said it, but I knew he did. He was always asking me how many times I'd felt the baby move each day and I always told him to stop fussing. Maybe if I'd have noticed she wasn't moving sooner, I could have got myself to hospital and saved her.'

'You couldn't have known,' he says in soothing tones, rubbing my back.

'Well, anyway. We didn't last long after that. Three months later he was with a new girlfriend and now she's pregnant.'

'Oh my God,' he gasps. I look up to see him reacting as if he's been punched in the stomach: hunched over, his eyes pained.

'Yeah, he moved on pretty quickly.' I notice that my

hands are shaking just re-telling it. 'Or at least that's how it felt for me at the time. I've since realised that he was just as devastated as me, but I was selfish. I wanted him to be in as much pain as me. So, you see, in a way, I'll never be over him. What we went through has bonded us forever.'

He throws me into a hug, his warm chest and the sound of his heartbeat calming me almost immediately.

'I'm so sorry that happened to you.'

'Don't you see? I'm screwed up because of it. It's left me with trust issues and that's before me falling for a man that was engaged to another woman. I'll forever be suspicious of you.'

He pulls me back by my shoulders, his earnest eyes penetrating mine. 'I don't care. I'll spend the rest of my life reassuring you that you're the only woman for me.'

What is it about his eyes that make me believe everything he tells me? It's probably more the fact that I'm in love with him.

'There's another thing, though.' I steel myself, trying to ready myself for his reaction. 'I know you want kids and… it's not that I don't want them, but I'm not sure if I can… you know, put myself through that again. What if it happened again? I wouldn't survive it the second time.' A sob escapes my mouth.

He shakes his head. 'I don't care. Whatever happens we're together. You're it for me, Nadine. Anything else is just a bonus.'

I smile, collapsing into his arms, feeling the safest and most loved I have in my entire life.

Two Years Later

I watch my flower girls walk down the aisle in front of me. Elizabeth, Hugh and Florence's daughter who I'm proudly godmother of; and Anna's daughter, Amelia. They're both over a year now and absolutely adorable. Between them they hold a balloon with Belle's name on it. My way of including her in our day.

A year ago, on Valentine's day, Hartley surprised me by filling our apartment with red roses and got down on one knee to propose with a heart-shaped, pink diamond ring. It was the happiest day of my life, but it's quickly being replaced by this one.

My page boys, Lydia and Jason's twin boys Carter and Benson, follow the girls down the aisle, shoving playfully at each other. The little rascals cause so much trouble wherever they go, but I love them so much. I couldn't have not involved them.

My bridesmaids: Mia, Kelly, Anna and Lydia, walk down next in their red-wine coloured, floor-length dresses, the pink personalised opal necklaces I bought them around their necks. They look amazing.

Anna's still living at my parents' house and managed to complete her GCSE's and AS Levels at a local college. It's been hard for her, but she's forever grateful that we gave her the option of keeping Amelia.

Her mum started visiting in secret when Amelia turned one but hasn't told her dad who is still adamant he wants nothing to do with her. Stupid fool.

With Hartley's surname being Valentine and him choosing Valentine's day to propose we decided to go into the theme rather than fight it. Is it cheesy? Of course, but it feels more personable to both of us.

'You ready?' Flo asks me, fluffing the train of my white lace dress. It's the first dress I tried on and I just knew instantly. From its V neckline with its illusion straps accented with lace appliques to its whimsical layers of dotted tulle and Chic organza. It was impossible for me not to fall in love with the vintage inspired beauty.

I smile back at her. 'More than ready.'

She gives me a quick hug. 'You look amazing, but then I did hear that someone with mad skills did your make up.' She winks and turns to walk down the aisle.

She really has made me look unbelievable. I have old Hollywood glamour red lips, the rest of my face mostly natural apart from the subtle gold sheen of eyeshadow that brings out my blue eyes.

Dad takes my arm. 'I'm so proud of you, my love.'

'Really?' I grin, holding on extra tight to my bouquet of pink and red peonies, different variations of pink and red roses, hypericum berries and eucalyptus. 'Even with the way we started?'

I still cringe when I think of us bumping into Dad in our upstairs hallway.

'Even with the way you started,' he nods. 'True love doesn't always have a smooth course, but you've made it. You're marrying the man of your dreams and I know he's going to do a good job looking after you.'

I really am.

The music changes to "Perfect" by Ed Sheeran, and Dad starts walking me down the aisle. Everyone turns in their seats to watch us descend, their faces illuminated in the candlelight. I can't help but feel terribly self-conscious, my cheeks heating, until I hear things like "stunning" and "beautiful". Then I spot him. My Hartley.

He turns, and everything feels one hundred percent better. He looks breathtaking in a navy-blue suit, his white shirt open at the collar. A single red rose is in his top pocket. He smiles at me as if I'm the only person in the room and my heart explodes.

The whole ceremony goes by fast and is a bit of a blur. Before I know what's happening we're walking back down the aisle and having heart shaped confetti thrown over us.

We make our way into the Duck and Goose reception room. Of course we had to have our wedding here. Hugh did some major grovelling after the fiasco that was Clara's wedding day and I'm now his official partner in the business.

Thankfully, Hugh's grandma had a word with her son and granddaughter Clara. Told them in no uncertain terms that they'd be written out of her will if she heard they'd been slagging off Hugh's business. I think her dad was so mortified by the whole thing he was glad to just forget about it. Hugh managed to eventually pay him back his money too, so he doesn't feel he owes him anything anymore.

Jill immediately hands us glasses of champagne with strawberry heart shaped ice cubes floating inside. I look around in triumph at the giant candelabras adorning the tables decorated with red and white roses. Love hearts are scattered over the tables like confetti. The name cards are written on Queen of Hearts playing cards. Heart shaped bunting made from pages of Romeo & Juliet, the play I helped Hartley with at this school, hangs from the ceiling. It's perfect.

We've gone for a laid back buffet with almost everything heart shaped: sandwiches, sausage rolls (who knew you could make them heart shaped!), mini pizzas (the first meal we shared together), and a chicken curry. Random I know, but it's all of our favourites and this way we know the kids will eat something.

The dessert table is where my heart really lies. It's adorned with heart shaped macarons, raspberry white chocolate cheesecakes, jam tarts; basically as many desserts as you can imagine, before you come across our wedding cake. It's white and simple, with matching flowers from my bouquet adorned on the side. But struck through it is a gold cupid's bow.

This whole wedding has been so close to being trashy and classless, but it's all tied together perfectly.

Hartley stops at our top table to kiss me again, his hand finding my stomach. I smile, but quickly push it away. We don't want anyone to know about our little miracle baby boy growing there.

We plan to announce it later tonight during the speeches. Of course, I'm scared the same thing will happen to him that happened to Belle, but according to the doctors there's only a two-point-five percent chance of it happening again. Don't get me wrong, that hasn't stopped me obsessing over it, but as Hartley says, that's ninety-seven-point-five percent chance of everything going fine. Of me holding my healthy baby boy in my arms and him growing up in a loving family home that me and Hartley created. Of telling him about his older sister Belle, who's soul was too beautiful for this earth. Of being able to tell him all about how I got to marry Mr Valentine.

Six Months Later

Mr & Mrs Valentine are over the moon to announce the birth of their baby boy,

Finley Everett Valentine

8 pounds, 6 ounces

THE END

Acknowledgements

Thanks so much for reading my book :-) If you enjoyed it I'd love if you took a few minutes to write a review on Amazon/Goodreads.

I'm so grateful for my family for their unwavering support. Without you guys and your craziness I'd have no material at all.

Thank you to everyone that made this book what it is. Andrea M Long for her editing skills and for being a friend I can turn to when I'm freaking out that what I've written is a pile of shit. Yummy By Design for doing another fabulous job with this book cover. I love it! Irish Ink Formatting for making this book look gorgeous. Especially when I send it over looking a mess!

Thanks a bunch to all of the bloggers and readers that take time out of their crazy schedules to share my posts, review and spread the word. Without you guys I'd be nothing.

Special thanks to my Indie Girls group. Always there for me whenever I need support only a fellow author can give.

Also by Laura Barnard

The Debt & the Doormat Series

The Debt & the Doormat

The Baby & the Bride

Porn Money & Wannabe Mummy

Babes of Brighton

Excess Baggage

Love Uncovered

Standalones

Tequila & Tea Bags

Dopey Women

Sex, Snow & Mistletoe

Heath, Cliffs & Wandering Hearts

Adventurous Proposal

Connect with Me

www.laurabarnardbooks.co.uk

www.facebook.com/laurabarnardbooks

https://twitter.com/BarnardLaura

https://www.instagram.com/laurabarnardauthor/